IN THE HEART OF THE DRAGON

By
ROBERT KIEHN

IN THE HEART OF THE DRAGON
Copyright © 2016 by ROBERT KIEHN

Library of Congress Control Number:		2016962873
ISBN-13:	Paperback:	978-1-63524-774-9
	PDF:	978-1-63524-775-6
	ePub:	978-1-63524-776-3
	Kindle:	978-1-63524-777-0

All rights reserved. No part of this publication may be reproduced, distributed, or transmitted in any form or by any means, including photocopying, recording, or other electronic or mechanical methods, without the prior written permission of the publisher or author, except in the case of brief quotations embodied in critical reviews and certain other noncommercial uses permitted
by copyright law.

Although every precaution has been taken to verify the accuracy of the information contained herein, the author and publisher assume no responsibility for any errors or omissions. No liability is assumed for damages that may result from the use of information contained within.

Printed in the United States of America

LitFire LLC
1-800-511-9787
www.litfirepublishing.com
order@litfirepublishing.com

Contents

Chapter 1 1

Chapter 2 17

Chapter 3 27

Chapter 4 46

Chapter 5 56

Chapter 6 82

Chapter 7 96

Chapter 8 113

Chapter 9 141

Chapter 10 165

Chapter 11 183

Chapter 12 207

Chapter 13 233

Chapter 1

At the Crossroads

"He who fights with monsters should see to it that he himself does not become a monster ... when you gaze long into the abyss, the abyss also gazes into you..."

-FREDRICK NIETZCHE

In the heart of the dragon lies agony, pain and deceit. The dragon has no mercy, devouring all that lay in its path. The dragon feeds on misery, perverts the truth and whispers his lies to the innocent. He appears as a friend to all and few recognize him for what he is. I know I have looked him in the eye and I also have failed like the many before me. I have just passed my thousandth moon in life, which has been more than enough in constant war with the dragon. I am old and desire rest but before I expire as an old and decrepit man I wish to give warning to others that follow. The wolves howl my name in the midnight hours, calling for my reckoning and the dragon mocks me my every step. My dreams haunt me through the night so that there is no peaceful rest.

This is the testimony of all that I know, beware. In recent years, dragons have been said to be sympathetic creatures, misunderstood and good once you get to know them. They are nothing of the sort. A dragon is pure concentrated evil; he only wants to you to think he is sincere. He sets his trap, then ambushes you in the night like a cheap wayward thief. Though dragons have razor sharp teeth, powerful talons and breathe fire, their real weapon is in subtlety. The dragon has always been after me, since the day I was born, chasing me and invading my very soul. Some say that dragons are not real, a faery tale made up to scare little children but they are real, alive and existing in the hearts of men. Feeding off sorrow, searing the soul and breaking the spirit. This is his day to reign, the dragon calls. I have looked the dragon in the eye, and he has won.

I walk in the shadows of life, fighting within my own heart to do that which is right. Someone once told me the greatest battle ever fought is the one that is waged within the mind... the battle within your own heart. But I have always lived for the moment, rarely considering consequences. I have never given much thought to the choices I have made until after it was too late. However, my soul is seared with the memories of this life and haunts my senses. To others I seem cold and distant. For myself, I yearn for more; to feel alive with emotions is something I have never experienced. To know love and passion seems too distant to be reality.

-Lord Thomas Kray, in the year 5006 p.d.

Consciousness drifted just beyond his reach. Echoes resounded within the cavern walls. The voices grew louder, demanding attention, but he was trapped somewhere, between past and present, between dream and life.

Securely bound by his feet and hands from the end of a rope, hanging upside down, Thomas could not move. The rope anchored to a post jutting out from the smooth sides of a volcano wall. The heat from below was unbearable; the sweat no longer dripped from his forehead and his mouth was as dry as a forsaken desert.

As he swayed to and fro near the apex of the pit, he could see the fiery glow of the molten rock nearly one thousand feet below. The scorched air stung at his lungs, he struggled for each breath through the smell of Sulphur. Flames belched upward from the depths. Squinting his eyes for protection, he tried to assess the situation. It was grim. He was in deep trouble. There was no help coming.

The walls of the volcano were as smooth as glass. Etched in the black wall, the image of a beast sneered down at him. The serpent-like dragon glared as if ready to consume his next victim. The etching was immense, sprawling across the entire width of the cavern wall. The eyes of the dragon were deep faceted rubies. Each scale of the serpent was carefully carved and inlaid with silver.

The etching glared at Thomas as if the beast knew that he was trapped without hope, an evil laugh resounded throughout the cavern. The snarling grin of the dragon carving mocked him victoriously. Ruby eyes flashed like lightening through the cavern. The laughter grew louder. Twisting about, frantically searching for the source of the laughter, he recognized a shadowy figure below. A tall, lanky man grinned crazily up at him. He was wearing a long white robe and wore his hair pulled back in a severe ponytail. It was his nemesis. He had won.

"Thomas, it's time we brought this battle of the minds to an end. This morning you will have fulfilled your purpose in life. You are so pathetic you don't even know what that purpose is! Well, I'll tell you…sacrifice! You will fulfill the prophecies, today! I shall release you from the bondage of this world, Thomas, you will find peace! You will finally soar…not with mere eagles, Thomas. You will reach far above the heavens, with the Master…you will fly with Dracos, through fire, and you will be set free! And I will watch you burn!" The man swept toward a cave opening. Pausing, he turned, and with a final grin, he sneered, "Don't go anywhere!" In an instant he was gone, and all was silent, with the exception of the pounding of Thomas's heart.

The man that put him there has the heart of a dragon. He would not know it if you asked him. He has not a clue that he is evil. Thomas's consciousness started to fade again, and he went back in time when he was younger, when it all started. It seemed like an eternity now. How long was it? Months? Years? He couldn't remember now.

Thunder echoed throughout the valley, lightning illuminated the night. A cold driving rain drenched the king's soldiers as they brought Thomas's father home on the back of a weary horse. A soldier held up a burning lamp. His father's armor clad body lay pale and still. Thomas reached for him and shuddered in horror when he saw the wounds that had stolen his life. The jagged remains of his flesh clung to his bones, his body chewed by some ghastly beast. A cleft in his shoulder blade went clear to his heart, made by the thorny stinger of the beasts he fought, the beasts that killed him. Several arrows stuck in his body were broken off at the shaft were and were not bothered for removal. The soldiers had made a hasty retreat in the night. Captain Arturas stood stone face before Thomas's mother, Lady Lauryn Kray.

Thomas and Arturas grew up together, Arturas was just two years older than he and Thomas grew up admiring and looking up to Arturas as a close friend. They went to school and played together. He was now gray haired and tired looking. The toil of war took its toll on him aging him long before his years. Arturas always had a great sense of humor and always had a way of making Thomas laugh. Now he looked bitter and strained, like a branch about to break under its own weight.

"I apologize for his condition, my Lady, we made a retreat and there was no time to prepare his body. We were completely routed. Our forces were superior to that of the dargons's, but our men stood frozen on the battlefield and were gripped by an abnormal fear. I believe there was some sort of black magic working against us that day. Dargons are unnatural, unholy creatures and come from the very depths of Hell itself."

Lady Kray broke down and began to wail, she fell to her knees and pulled at the grass, Captain Arturas ordered his men to cover up her husband's body and they quickly obeyed. Thomas stood, staring at his father's covered corpse. He didn't cry, he stood unmoving not knowing what to say or do.

One of the soldiers stood before Lady Kray, Thomas recognized him, and he was not much older than he was but his hair was already turned gray as well. His armor had many dents; he was bleeding and dirty. It was Will Grayson, he was a freckle faced boy growing up and now he looked weary too. "We loved and respected your husband, Lady Lauryn, we'll do what we can to help", he said.

Thomas had no beard on his face as of yet and he was wondering if would ever come in, but he was strong and good with a bow. He was brash, full of ideals and slightly foolish. Looking forward to his turn in battle, a test of a man's true mettle or so he thought. He longed for adventure and fight the evil horde that came from the west islands. Captain Arturas approached him; he was his father's most trusted officer and his second in command. He handed him his father's sword, a large two-handed piece that was as long as Thomas was tall; the haft was inlaid with gold and was crafted by the king's own armorer. The steel glowed in the night as if it gave off its own light. He turned it over in his hand admiring the craftsmanship, he could barely wield it but the heaviness felt good to him.

"This belongs to you now," the captain said. "Your father died bravely, Thomas. He was the only one who did not lose his courage in battle. All would have been lost if not for him. He rallied his men and led the charge. It broke the spell on the soldier's minds, but it was too late. Too many were cut down by those vile savages."

"Thank you," he said feebly. "I will try to live up to my father's name."

"It is time that you set out on your own and make a name for yourself, Thomas." He handed him a leather pouch and mounted his steed. "The Citadel of Orinkur is fallen, the dargons have sacked it, their vile stench has infested that beautiful city. Vile blood has soaked the ground and made it unlivable." He called to the handful of men that remained of his fathers; Arturas was now their leader. "Come," he called out to them, "we must prepare to defend the castle, there are dark times ahead."

Thomas's mother, sobbing gently, led the horse to a glen behind the stone built house, where all of his generations laid in rest, returning to the soil. Small stone markers told of their deaths. He helped her with the body of Lord Holden Kray and built a pile of wood, they clumsily placed him atop of the funeral pyre. She anointed his body with oil and sprinkled his body with herbs, two coins she placed on his eyes and with a lump of a coal she made the marking of a strange rune on his chest. Lady Lauryn was still deeply rooted in the old pagan ways and traditions, of which his father did not approve but tolerated because he loved his wife, it was good that he could not see what she was doing to him. His father had just converted to some mystical religion that had been sweeping through the countryside. His mother clung to the old ways. Thomas kept neither faith and relied on his own resources. Religion was for the weak. They lit the fire and watched as it burned. The fire grew and the colors and hues changed in the stormy night, first warm yellows and oranges then it changed to a twinkle of blue green. They stood there for hours watching as his father corpse was reduced to ashes, and the bones twisted and split. His sightless eyes stared back at Thomas. Lady Kray got down on her knees again and began to sing a song, Thomas recognized only a few of the words for it was in the tongue of the ancients.

> Koemyr, king and Lord of the deep
> Take this soul for thine to keep
> Silver the moon so full and bright
> Make his heart pure with light
> Cross the river, over summer's dell,
> Take this soldier, who in battle fell.

He could not understand much, for it was in the language of the mages and he understood only a little. To be honest he lost interest in her chanting, his mind was on what adventures might lie ahead, looking forward to setting out on his own. Captain Arturas sparked in him the yearnings for a quest, to find a riches and win the heart of a fair maiden. Lord Kray had been knighted, but he was not wealthy and the farm that they lived on was too boring for Thomas.

Walking home afterward, he surveyed the farmhouse that his father built through the dim light of the evening. It was made of stone with a thatched roof, as were all the houses in the village, aptly named Greystone because of the quarry and the coloration of the rocks. Now run down from lack of care, cold and drafty, the roof leaked, the inside offered little comfort.It was seven years since the war between humans and the dargons broke out. Thomas's father was only home briefly during that time. He lit a lamp and went to his room, placing all his belongings in his backpack, which was not very much. A bedroll, a tinderbox and the leather bag that his father had left to him. He could hear his mother gently sobbing in her room. Thomas slept fitfully for only a few hours and woke before sunrise; he grabbed his pack and set out.

Walking along a rocky road, wondering what his life was offering on ahead, he set out early in the morning, before his mother woke, not saying goodbye. She would only want to stop him, saying that she would need him, and he did not want to burden himself with the guilt. Knowing in his heart that he would not look again upon this run down farm that had barely sustained them through the winter, while his father was off on his campaigns in the north. Looking for the first time in the leather pouch Captain Arturas gave him, he found more gold then he had ever set his eyes upon. There were precious gems, and platinum coins along with a gold dagger that was obviously of ogre design. He wondered where his father had come upon this wealth. Had he been saving it all this time to bring home or did he just recently acquire it at his last battle? Why had he not sent it home? It didn't matter now it was Thomas's. At the bottom of all the coins lay a book, He flipped it open, but he could barely read and it gave him a headache just thinking about it. He threw back into his backpack; it did look important for in the back it contained a maps. He would hold on to it for now, maybe someone could explain it to him later.

He slung his father's sword across his back, sheathed and ready for trouble. He carried his bow in his hand and the dagger tucked in his belt along with the gold. He was ready to take on any adventure. He set off due east, away from the castle away from the people he had always known. Thomas wanted to make a mark on the world, on his own. He set off east for no particular reason. He had heard much about the cities of the east; his father spoke much of them. Lord Kray had traveled much through the land of Kuradur. Past where the eastern road ended, his father told him there was land still unexplored past the Kuradurians, a vast jungle where explorers dared to venture but never returned. To the west lay a desert, desolate and dry. Thomas was once near that barren wasteland to trade for horses with his father, long before the Second Dargon War, no one who attempted to cross that desert ever returned either. To the north lay the citadel of Orinkur, recently sacked by the dargon hordes, and past that was the Great Blue. To the south, more ocean. So east it was, for the time in this season. Maybe when he earned enough money he could book passage and sail across the southern sea or better yet, buy a ship of his own. The eastern road told of fortune, dragons and wizards. A man could even make a living on killing ogres for hire or even thieving from them.

Ogres were great ugly beasts that looked humanistic but were twice the size, luckily they were dumber than rocks and there were only a few. Ogres preferred the flesh of humans; they roamed outside the cities of the east in small bands. They liked gold and trinkets and kept all the loot from their victims. Otherwise the dargons were a nasty lot, small six legged creatures that looked a cross between a rat and some insect that should be squashed under your moccasin. They came from across the great blue on an island country they quickly outgrew. There were thousands of them, in battle they outnumbered humans six to one but they died easily with one whack of your sword. They had no sense of money or trade, but devoured the fallen in the fray. Their leaders, the trolls, on the other hand, walked on two feet and carried trophy human skulls strung to their belt. In combat the trolls would their arrows loose from the rear.

Thomas continued on his journey, the citadel had fallen, but what of his mother, what would become of her? She would need the money his father had left to move away and set up a new farm safe from danger. It would not be long before those vile beings started to infest their way to Greystone. The pangs of guilt began to overtake Thomas, there was more gold than he would need and he had the means to make more. Thomas couldn't believe his selfishness. Coming to a fork in the road, the crossroad at Nightsbridge Forest, he turned on his heels. Walking fast a first, he switched to a long quick stride. He could hurry back, leave her most of the gold and kiss her goodbye. Why was he so foolish to be so brash, he asked himself? If he was lucky, she might not even be worrying yet. Looking up he could see the smoke in the distance; he stopped cold in his tracks. His heart fell to his stomach and he began to run like he had never done before.

The house was engulfed in flames; the barn lay in smoldering ruins, crackling and sending sparks into the air. The animals all lay dead on the ground.Searching franticly for his mother, he opened the door to the house without thinking. There was an explosion that knocked him ten feet into the yard.He turned his head to answer a whispered plea. Lying against a tree, was his mother, her clothes were torn and she was nearing death. Scrambling to reach her, Thomas scooped his mother into his arms. Her body was badly bruised and her face was ashen, life was ebbing from her body, she could not move.

"Mother," Thomas cried. "What has happened?" His head sank low, and he stared into the grass. "What have I done?"

"There were six of them," she said weakly. "They came at dawn and burst through the doors, they tore the house to pieces searching for something. I know not what they were looking for. When they could not find it they set the house on fire and beat me. They headed west looking for you, thank the goddess's that you are still alive, I was so worried for you. There was another one with them, he was tall and dark..."

But that was all that she could say and she died there in his arms. Cradling her body Thomas brought her to a woodpile, placing the body gently upon it, just outside of the burning home. He made sure it was lit, it was the way she would have wanted it, although he skipped the ritual canting.

Stumbling to the front gate, Thomas reeled from guilt, his stomach turned sour and he wretched against the gatepost. Composing himself, he noticed a purple scrap of satin. Snatching it from the briars, he turned it over in his hands. Noting the fine red embroidery, he had seen this somewhere before. Falling to his knees, he vowed to avenge his mother. Stuffing the fabric swatch into his pouch with the gold pieces, securing his father's sword upon his back, Thomas refused to ever look back.

His vengeance seethed within him, and he began to run towards the town of Greystone by the back trails. He had moved, undetected throughout these back wood trails for many years, hunting and trapping with his father. He knew every shortcut. The sweat was pouring down upon his face as he crept into the town of Greystone. It was a cool day, but he was hot with the fire of hatred. Thomas was not battle hardened and he was severely outnumbered. He considered none of these things, he only wanted revenge. Thomas knew he could probably take down one or two of the enemy before they got to him. Adrenaline was surging through his brain; he was perched at the village wall, ready to attack. However, there seemed to be no one around. The small burg was deadly quiet. He drew out his bow; cautiously searching the streets and shops, hugging the small thatched homes made of stone and mud. The blacksmith's house was abandoned, his fire still burning out front. Approaching the Crimsonstar Tavern Thomas looked inside; the sign hanging over the door creaked as he peaked inside the window. He could see the innkeeper cowering behind his bar. Thomas knew him well; his name was Tolson Aleman. His son, Braxton and Thomas were friends since their youth. Tolson was a big man with the courage of a newborn kitten. He entered the tavern with caution.

"Are they gone boy?" Tolson asked. Thomas looked at him questioningly. "The soldiers in red chain mail on horseback are they still here?" he began to relax and came out from behind the bar. "Evil looking they were; I couldn't see their faces. They didn't look human." the barkeep added in a long sigh.

"Did any of them have purple satin on that looked like this?" Thomas held out the purple swatch of cloth he had found at the gate of his house.

Mr. Aleman examined it closely. "Aye, they all did underneath the saddles of their horses, it had a picture of a red dragon upon it. Evil they were," he repeated. "You could smell it on them, smelt like the smithies fire. Tore through this town looking for something or someone. Kilt anyone who tried to escape. They shot arrows right through their hearts, they did, made a funny hissing noise when they hit, poisoned tips I reckon."

"Where's Braxton?" Thomas said worriedly. He was a great friend and now he was the only friend he had.

"He's alright, he's upstairs, wanted to go out and fight them all by his lonesome till I reminded him he didn't have a weapon to fight them with. Paced back and forth like he was some kind of a warrior. Took me forever to talk some sense into him. Thank the gods they're gone. They are gone, aren't they?"

"I think they're gone now. Did you see where they left to Mister Aleman?"

"Are you kiddin me, I didn't leave comforts of being behind that bar. I drank my best stout and prayed to the goddess Moriah to save my own skin. I ain't no glory seek'n hero. They ransacked this place and took off. Laughed like madmen when they saw me underneath the counter."

Walking upstairs, he could hear Braxton muttering to himself. "If only I had a sword. I could of showed them something there was only ten of them..."

As much as Tolson Aleman was a coward, his son, Braxton tried to make up for it in bravery. He often got into fights to prove that he wasn't his father. His father was not only a coward, but he was also a drunk and a lousy businessman. Braxton strived to be more than his father ever was, but he always loved him unconditionally.

At age seventeen he was as big, or bigger than his father was. Brax worked for his father but also as an apprentice to the blacksmith, he was quite strong and muscular. Braxton took pride in being a fighter, and turned red with humiliation and anger when the townsfolk snickered over his father being yellow. The boy could easily knock out two or three full-grown men, especially if he were angry enough. Braxton never admitted defeat, and never stopped or backed down, even if he were outnumbered.

"I could of taken them all, easily." He continued.

"Who are you talking to, Brax?"

"Thomas, you should have been here, there were strange soldiers that pillaged Greystone. Together we could of taken them. My wits, your bow, they would of been dead where they stood." He stopped, looking at Thomas. "Isn't that your fathers' sword?" He asked.

"My father was killed in the Northern Campaign against the dargons, Captain Arturas delivered it to me last night, along with all of his belongings. My mother was killed this morning by the same devils that came through town today. I've sworn to myself get every last one of them, I'm going after them."

"I'll be going with you. You and I together, adventure as last!"

"Agreed, but what will your father say?"

"Thomas, I'm nearly a man and as big as one. I can seek my own way and to Hades with this little town, I'm going to see the world. I even have some money stashed away."

By now the timid town's people started to venture out of their homes and into the streets. A vendor picked up his fruit and futilely tried to salvage what was left, the coppersmith banged out the dents of his pots and pans, another swept out the debris from his destroyed general store. Braxton and Thomas walked out of the Crimsonstar and into the dirt street; raw sewage trickled in a gutter on the side. A woman was sobbing holding her dead husband in the dirt road. The smell of death clung in the air of the late afternoon.

Kneeling to the ground, Thomas examined the tracks made by the horses. "They split up, five headed east and five headed west."

"Where do we go?" asked Braxton.

"We go east, it's where I was going anyway." he said, "Besides, there's money to be made in the east, running bounties and trading. Past Everhall there's nothing but desert."

"I need to buy a sword, Thomas, without one I'll be as much use as stray dog."

We headed to the blacksmiths shop where Conus Biggers made his metal wears. Conus mostly made shoes for plow horses but he did make a few weapons now and again for the passing adventurer. He made painstakingly careful swords folded and hardened from the finest steel.

"Conus, I need to buy a sword, one of your best."

Conus looked at him and laughed, "You can't afford it boy, now get lost."

"Can you give me a deal, as an old friend and former employee?"

"You see this sword? It took me six months to make, I don't make deals and you still cannot afford what I've got." He looked down on Braxton. "So you're finally leaving town after all your talk."

"I've got fifty silver pieces, old man, what'll that get me?"

Conus went into his store and came back with a black long knife with a wooden handle, it was pitted and hardly had an edge that could cut.

"That thing, you sell those to the farmers to cut the corn, you old coot. What about the stainless steel one hangin' on your wall?"

"That is the finest sword I have ever made, I folded over one hundred time, I inured it in the purest mountain stream from the Muse Mountains. It took me over a year to make it. No, not for fifty lousy silver pieces."

"How about ten in gold?" Thomas interrupted.

He looked him and laughed again but stopped when he spotted the money in Thomas's hand and saw that he was not joking. "Sold, my friend."

Braxton and Thomas walked back to Crimsonstar Inn. "Thankya Thomas, for the sword I mean. Tis a sure fine one at that." He said turning over in his hands slowly. "It's got a good feel in me hands."

"Think nothin of it, if we're going to be traveling together I need you to be armed with the best that there is. Let's get something to eat at your father's, I've had nothing since morning."

"I'm starved me self, but I wanted to make a clean break, he'll try and talk me out of it."

"I'm not leaving till I've had something in my stomach, and Aleman's roast mutton sounds like it would hit the spot."

After a hearty meal Braxton gathered his meager belongings into a small knapsack. Walking downstairs his father confronted him, "And where do ya think you're a goin?"

"Adventurin'...with Thomas."

"Are ya bloody daft, boy? The two of you get lost travelin' to the outhouse, you'll come cryin' back here like a coupla' whelps, or you'll get yurself kilt, and then what use would you be to me. It's not like I'm young anymore, I ain't gonna make anymore of you."

"We're go'in to get those devils on horseback, Da', they kilt Thomas's ma and we're going after em."

"Nope, no you're not going anywhere. Your stayin' right her, now go get a broom and clean this mess up in here."

"I'm going, and you cannot stop me. I got me a sword."

"Oho, look at you, all full of yourselves and puffed up. What more could you want. How about a brain?"

Braxton looked down. "I'm need'n the rest of me wages."

"So that's it, ok boy, but when you get yourself kilt don't come cry'in back to me. Here's what's owed you."

"Da, this here's more than what's owed."

"Shut up son, don't go ruin a moment. Get some food, there's jerked meat in the kitchen and some bread. Take what's stale now, the fresh stuff's for payin' customers."

"Thanks Da," Braxton hugged his father and they set out upon the eastern road.

Chapter 2

The Prevailing Myst

Like one who, on a lonely road, Doth walk in fear and dread,And, having once turned round, walks on, And turns no more his head;Because he knows a frightful fiend Doth close behind him tread.

-Coleridge, The Ancient Mariner

Thomas and Braxton departed Greystone with high expectations. Braxton imagined fighting ogres and trolls as he slashed his way through the open air with both hands on his shiny new sword. Thomas dreamed of gold, elaborate palaces, and what lay in the East, they strutted along the road with complete confidence. They spoke of many things along the way, their pace was strong and the strides were long, making good time upon the open road. Thomas's thoughts turned once again to his mother, his furrowed brow crinkled and Braxton knew that it was time to be quiet. He knew when Thomas was angry, he was best left alone. They walked on in silence, Braxton took a pull from his goatskin flask, it was water mixed with a little wine. His father proved to be a far more practical advisor for traveling then Braxton could imagine. He gave them two flasks, dried meat and fruit, rope and an assortment of tools and knives; giving Braxton the feeling that maybe his father was neither ignorant of traveling or adventuring.

Thomas brooded until they came upon the crossroad, near Nightsbridge Forest, where he had suddenly decided to turn back earlier that morning; it was now late in the day and unusually hot for early spring. He could feel a few blisters forming on his tender feet, he was not used to the long trek. They decided to camp there for the night, heading to the woods for cover. Braxton started a fire and Thomas set out to find fresh game, deciding it best to save the jerked meat when food was scarcer. It did not take him long and he soon came trotting back proudly with a rabbit he took.

"You should have seen the shot, Brax, a hundred yards, if not an inch more. Sometimes I amaze myself."

"You don't need an audience Thomas, you'll always have your biggest fan with you, yourself." Braxton chided but he knew that the brag was probably true. Thomas could out shoot anyone with the longbow; it was like he was born to it. Sprinkling a little powder into a hallowed out portion of a fallen limb, he rubbed it with a stick until it burst into flames. Braxton had done this many times at the Crimson Star Inn to get the ovens going for his father. Brax was happy that one of the few skills he brought with him on this quest was starting a fire along with the ability to cook. He expertly cleaned the rabbit, put it on spit and covered in herbs; another provision made by the elder Aleman. Their first night out and everything seemed just fine, they were handling themselves like professional rangers, or so they imagined.

The night came suddenly and without much warning, both would be adventurers realized why the forest was named Nightsbridge. They had settled for the night deep into the woods in a clearing, counting on the cover to protect from an ambush. The clearing told of a religion long forgotten, it was surrounded by large oblong rocks placed in a circle. In the center was an altar, Thomas laid his bedroll down beside it to fitfully tossed and turned for the rest of the night. He could not get his mind off the day's events, his mother died in his arms over and over again. The purple scrap of satin sash and the ten riders was a mystery. "What did they want with me and my mom?" he asked himself aloud. It was so deafeningly quiet even Thomas's thoughts seemed to echo and shatter the night.

He pulled his blanket close as the night became colder, he tossed and turned, a thousand troubling thoughts ran through his mind.

Braxton's snoring helped little. Thomas felt uneasy and peered out across the opening in the woods. A mist enveloped them in billows, as if a great beast were exhaling nearby.

"Of all the luck." Thomas muttered to himself, pulling his bedroll around him even tighter, the cold mist settling into his bones.

The fog came in thick, obscuring his vision. Thomas couldn't see his hand in front of his face andsilently ten dark riders, with purple satin horse blankets, passed by on the road.

Giving up their search because they could no longer follow the trail left by Thomas and Braxton, ten riders of the Order of the Hammer stopped along the road. Black Uhr, the leader of the ten riders, was assigned this mission because of his expertise in tracking. Uhr was from Kojan, an island full of mystics, beggars, and mercenaries. His mission was to locate the offspring of the dark haired warrior, Lord Kray. Black Uhr was in the employ of the Wizards Guild who contracted the Order of the Hammer to carry out less than appropriate deeds. The Order of the Hammer were battle scarred old men and The Prince's favorite mercenaries. Black Uhr could track anything day or night, but this mere boy eluded him. The boy's trail had led around in a big circle, from the Nightsbridge crossroad, then back to his home and through Greystone. He divided his team of twenty, sending ten men with Odin in charge to the western city Storm Gap, and himself with nine others to Cross Falls. They were bound to turn up in one of those two cities, for no fool would go north where the besieging forces of the dargons were now spreading. Now with all the luck, a mist was developing so thick he could not see the trail; let alone any signs of tracks. He lost all sign of Thomas and his unknown friend that accompanied him.

Black Uhr took the road southeast, which eventually led to Mission Keep. He motioned silently for his team to come to halt. The riders, lost in the fog, not paying attention, collided with their leader, breaking the silence of the night.

"Buffoons!" Black Uhr lurched to maintain control of his mount on the majestic black steed. He swung about and cursed into the night. He dismounted swiftly and knelt to the ground, sniffing the earth. "I've lost the trail. We can backtrack or we can head on, my sense tells me to head to Mission Keep. I believe this troublesome boy Thomas Kray and his companion are heading there."

"The great Black Uhr has lost the scent, my how the mighty can fall."

Without saying a word or showing any sign of emotion, Black Uhr carefully walked to the insolent man. Through the mist he could not rely on his sense of sight but when he knew he was close, he shot out his hand, deftly grabbing hold of Borgman and jerked him off his horse sending him clattering down to the ground. The other riders wisely choosing not to get involved with in the altercation between the mercenary from Kojan and Borgman. The rest of the riders were silently fearful of Black Uhr, who stood almost seven feet tall and had dark blue scaly skin that made him appear like a lizard. In fact, a lizard was the best way to describe Black Uhr's appearance. He usually had his cloak pulled around his face to avoid disturbance, but when he took it off, it showed he had no ears, nor hair.

"You fool," Borgman spat, "What happened to your orders of strict silence."

"You have already shattered the noise discipline when you so adeptly crashed into the rear of my horse, dolt."

Black Uhr's second in command, Borgman, was a human. Black Uhr held disdain for Borgman, not only because he was an inept clod but also he could not understand how the human could so easily betray a member of his own race. A few gold coins and Borgman would sell out his own mothers. Borgman was chosen by the dark wizard named The Prince to tag along with Black Uhr. He thanked the lord Jagen that The Prince was no longer with them, the wizard was powerful and even gave Black Uhr cause to worry. The Prince's temper was legendary, he would send out a spell killing the closest and most hapless person, although usually it was no one of any importance. A servant girl or eunuch was a common target; he rarely destroyed someone of importance unless they really screwed up. Borgman was The Prince's political advisor, and one of his favorites, it seemed The Prince cherished sycophants more than men with ability.

"Who is this other person, is he someone we have to worry about?" Borgman said as he picked himself up and dusted himself off. Borgman either never held a grudge or just acted like nothing ever bothered him. He flashed a wry grin.

Black Uhr's pursed mouth wrinkled as if he smelled something foul. The ability of politics was lost upon the Kojan; there were no grays, only black and white. "There is much I can tell from a footprint on the ground, someone's identity is not one of them. He is one hundred ninety-six pounds but that is subject to how much weight he is carrying, about six foot in height, he is light on his feet but makes no effort to hide his trail. By the breadth of his print he is probably very young. My guess he is only a friend of Thomas Kray's. His ability with the sword remains to be seen."

"Sword? How do you know he has a sword?"

"He nicked the trail a few times with it. My guess he was playing with it."

Borgman held a knack for winning over the hearts and minds of the masses, but he mistrusted Black Uhr. Mainly, the only reason for his doubt of Black Uhr was his appearance, which is ironic, for as a race the Kojan are incapable of deceit. Their warrior code was a complex mix of chivalry and honor, breaking the code meant a death sentence. However, they did not believe that their moral code applied to the human race and they often hired themselves out as mercenaries because of their love of warfare. Really, the fact that the Kojans had leathery blue skin and no visible ears was not the reason humans mistrusted them, but because of their forked tongues. When Black

Uhr pulled his cloak around his face, he appeared to be very human. The Kojan were few in number and in Greystone they were only heard of in stories. They came from far across the South Sea of Peace; they were nomadic by nature, loved to travel and were accomplished seamen.

"Maybe we should turn back and stay in Greystone for the evening."

"There is no reason to turn back. There is nothing for him, now that we burned his home and lands to the ground. It is only a matter of time before they wind up in Cross Falls." The clinging mist made Borgman shiver and he pulled his own cloak tighter to his body.

Black Uhr knew the real reason was that Borgman wanted to turn back was because he preferred sitting in a pub and drinking beer than being on the open road. Perhaps he was right though, the two hunted boys would eventually wind up in Cross Falls and they could lay a trap for them there. If they wound up in Cross Falls before the hunting party did, they could purchase horses giving them an edge in traveling and they could lose them. A good hunter knew that sometimes it was best to set a trap and wait for the prey to come to the bait. It would take hours to find the trail again; they would have to wait for the mist to clear until morning.

"I might remind you that even though you are in charge of this hunting party, I sit on the high wizard's council. When this is done and we have the key in our possession I might be able to appoint you to a position of trust."

"Your bribe is unnecessary; I have already made up my mind to head to east river crossroads. However, we ride on through the night and day till we get there. We must arrive there well before they do and lay a snare for them."

"Ride on through the night without rest! In this mist? Are you insane?"

"Come, we ride." Black Uhr did not leave Borgman space for debate. To hell with his position and his politics. When this deed was over, he was buying his own ship and he would be done with this human race forever.

Thirty miles to the west Odin Harbinger walked his horse through the small outpost village between Greystone and Everhall, the clip clop of the horses hooves hitting the cobblestone echoed through the night. Odin hadn't a clue as to the name of the village, for it was not even on the map. Honestly he didn't care, it was extremely late, chilly and he cared nothing more than to have a bed for the night and a hot toddy. Grumbling to himself so as the others could not hear, "Why has The Prince sent members of the ministry on some wild search for this key? I am too old and too cold to be gallivanting around the countryside, throughout the four regions. No one even knows the purpose for this key, aside from The Prince. What could be so important about it?"

"You would think the minister of defense was a more important person to stay in Mission Keep." He said louder this time.

"My lord?" His aide de camp asked. "Did you something?"

"No I didn't, now mind your business." He replied gruffly.

His aide would turn him over to The Prince for heresy for his own gain if he heard him complaining. Trotting tiredly up to the one and only inn, the riders tied their horses and went inside. It was well after midnight and they had to rouse the innkeeper.

"We don't get travelers this way so late in the year. Or this late at night for that matter." The innkeeper said curiously eyeing the swords the men were carrying. "What brings you gentleman this way, Everhall will not even be open for trade at this time?"

"None of your bloody business." Odin said so gruffly the fat little innkeeper didn't utter another word to him. Odin, with the grace of a newborn cow, walked up the stairs to his room. He fell asleep easily on the straw stuffed mattress; he would worry about interrogating the town's people on the whereabouts of the boy in the morning. One good thing, he was grateful for splitting up in Greystone. That Kojan, Black Uhr, gave him the creeps and was glad to be no longer with him. He was also glad to be rid of Borgman; he did not mind it so much that he raped that woman back on that pathetic farm but the way he beat her within an inch of her life made even his old battle weary stomach turn. Borgman got a full description from that lady of her son but it enraged Borgman when she didn't know where he was heading. Truly, Odin believed her she said she thought he was still at home.

Antonin, Odin's aide, was a bit more tactful with the innkeeper. "Here is your money kind sir, we will each have our own room that is if it's possible."

The innkeeper was elated, and his face brightened after the brush he had with the lanky gray bearded fellow, the inns business at this time of year was unheard of and the man was paying in gold no less. "Certainly, there are plenty of rooms available for all five of you. Take your pick."

"Pay no heed to the old man, he is eternally grumpy."

"T'is not a problem sir."

"Tell me, I have a friend I am trying to catch up with, he might be here, or passed through this quaint village. He's a young boy, about eighteen, nineteen years of age, tall too. Might you have seen him?"

"No one's passed through here for the past week. Old man Aleman and his boy came here with a delivery of beer but other than that no one."

"Alright then, we will be heading up to our beds too then."

"Thank you, sir, and goodnight to you, like I said it's pleasure to have you here, we don't get many people here at this time of year and they usually don't pay to get their own rooms, everyone normally doubles up to save money."

In the far off distance Thomas heard a loud crash, he slowly and cautiously rested his hand upon the hilt of his father's sword. Somewhere in the middle of his thoughts he had managed to fall asleep. His weariness did not make him aware that it was the riders. He listened attentively for a few minutes but quickly fell back asleep.

In the morning Thomas awoke with a start, Braxton was already awake and fixing breakfast. The two ate hastily and in silence. Throwing their packs on, they walked out of the woods.

Unfortunately, neither one of the 'would be' adventurers knew the lay out of the land having never ventured out of Greystone. Thomas knew the woods surrounding Greystone but he never went much farther past the confines of the hundred acres around his home. The land, along with the title of lord is what Thomas's father, Holden Kray, received for his bravery in the first war against the dargons. Greystone was a small principality on the outskirts of the land of Corrin, not like the great cities like Mission Keep or the Citadel Orinkur, their town was smaller than any other of the four kingdoms. Thomas knew this from the tales that his father told him late in the evenings by the fire of a winter's night. He told him of his battles during the war that lasted over four years, hunting down every last one of the dargons and the beasts that controlled them, but now the beasts had returned. Holden was no more than a sergeant at the onset of the war, but when the commander was killed during a battle, Holden Kray automatically took over, leading his men to cut off the retreat of the dargons. Returning to Greystone he received a hero's welcome, and for this he received the title and the land. It was gift from the people of Greystone for keeping their honor.

Greystone was without a lord for many years. He died in the middle of the night after a long illness. He was young and left no heirs.

Some suspect that he was poisoned but no one knew from whom. Many people died for no explainable reasons, kings and queens were no exceptions. Death comes for the wicked and honorable, the poor and the rich, the weak and the strong. Death came for Thomas's family without a notice.

Chapter 3

Pirates, Thieves or Soldiers

Hear my soul speak. Of the very instant that I saw you, did my heart fly at your service.

-William Shakespeare. The Tempest.

Thomas woke early in the morning, and the mist was still all around and there was a chill in the air. He tried to curl up more inside his blanket for warmth but he still shivered like the last brown leaf clinging to a tree in the wind. In the mist he saw two eyes like hot embers in a fire, the mist swirled around in a tempest. Out from the depths of the mist came a dragon, fierce and angry. He breathed and flame came from his pursed lips, not a violent flame as one would expect, but a gentle one that flickered blue and made a light crackling sound. His scales shimmered gray as if he was reflecting the mist. Golds, blues, and silvers twinkled off his skin like a starry night. A toilsome trouble at the end of a dog night, the dragon came to haunt him. Larger, larger he grew with each breath he took, twisting and twisting, snarling and snarling, and then he was gone. Thomas woke, it was a dream, nothing but a dream and there was no mist, the sun creeped up over the trees and he realized it was late morning and they over slept.

They ate a quick breakfast then Thomas and Brax continued on with their journey and they were feeling pretty cheerful despite the tragedies of the past days. They marched along the trail as if they were soldiers, holding their swords across their shoulders. Thomas started singing a song he learned from Arturas before he had marched off for war in the north.

Ole King Knod,

Was a mighty fine sod,

He called for his fife, and called for his knife,

And he called for his privates three,

Ohhh! I don't want go to war said the privates,

But a merry ole men are we,

Oh the others are fine but you can't compare,

The King's infantry!

Ole King Knod,

Was a mighty fine sod,

He called for his fife, and called for his knife,

And he called for his corporals three,

Beer, beer, beer yelled the corporals,

But a merry ole men are we,

Oh the others are fine but you can't compare,

The King's infantry!

Ole King Knod,

Was a mighty fine sod,

He called for his fife, and called for his knife,

And he called for his sergeants three,

War, war, war called the sergeants,

But a merry ole men are we,

Oh the others are fine but you can't compare,

The King's infantry!

Ole King Knod,

Was a mighty fine sod,

He called for his fife, and called for his knife,

And he called for his captains three,

Everyone get in line ordered the captains,

But a merry ole men are we,

Oh the others are fine but you can't compare,

The King's infantry!

At the end of each verse, Thomas and Brax turned to each other and saluted, laughing all the way down the twisted path.

Ole King Knod,

Was a mighty fine sod,

He called for his fife, and called for his knife,

And he called for the Sergeant Major,

Ohhh! Everyone better fall in yelled the Sergeant Major,

But a merry ole man am I,

You can have your war, you can have your beer,

But you'd better listen to me!

Brax turned to Thomas and bowed deeply. "Why thank you, sir, that was a very fine performance, I must insist."

"No thank you." Said Thomas bowing as well. "T'was your voice that that carried the true talent."

"Aye, but without you it would never have happened."

"True, too true."

"So Thomas, I hate to be a pest but where exactly are we going?"

Thomas paused, put down his sword and peered off in to the east. He pondered a moment stroking his chin as if deep in thought. "That way." He said pointing to the east.

"Well that's good, for a minute there I was thinking you didn't have a plan. Where east, do tell?"

"I don't have a plan. None at all."

"Nothing!"

"The basic plan is to head east, there's ogres to the east. We could plunder their riches, they're known to horde gold and rum."

"Ogres are also eight feet tall and tear a human apart limb from limb, like they were tearing petals away from a flower, then they grind your bones and use your head for a football."

"That seems a little exaggerated." Said Thomas. "Ogres are pretty fat and slow."

"I'm going to err on the more cautious side."

"We could become pirates."

"Do you know how to sail, Thomas?"

"No, but I hear that pirates have a great training program."

"They also tend lose their legs and have to walk around on a peg leg, or they get hanged for piracy. Do you know what they do to pirates when they catch them? They put them in cage until they starve to death, and as they sail past other pirate's point, look, and say, there's poor Tom, he used to be a man of flesh and blood but now he's just bones."

"Every job has its risks, Brax. Every adventure, every quest is not going to be safe. If you want to be safe, then go back home. Aye a pirate's life seems like it could be fun, few rules and lots of mayhem."

"Just saying, maybe we could join the Army. I know it's not safe but we'll get steady pay."

"I don't see myself in the Army Brax."

"Why not?"

"I never followed orders well, plus my I tend to say things out loud when I shouldn't. You remember what I said to the Science teacher when he said the world was carried on the back of giant bear?"

"Yeah, you said 'it seems like it would be a really bumpier ride, and I don't feel nothing.'"

"Exactly, and I got in trouble the teacher, my mother, and principle. Seems to me they should have been teaching us to read."

"Ain't nobody knows how to read these days."

"Someone must. I have this book and I don't even know what it is."

"Yeah well, I don't think you need to read for all the adventuring we're going to be doing."

"Maybe so, but I still think knowing how to read would come in handy."

"You worry too much."

"I still don't want to join the Army. You'll never get rich joining the Army."

"Who cares about being rich. I want to be famous. I want people to look at my statue and say 'there's Brax, hero of the Four Corners."

"Heroes are usually dead."

"Of course they are, but they're remembered, and that's an eternity of sorts."

"I suppose you're right Brax, from the onset of my life I fear I was created for obscurity. Twenty years from now I don't want to look around and say to myself I've accomplished nothing. I want to make a mark on life."

"I want to make a mark to, a big mark."

"Stop!"

"What is it?" Brax asked.

"You have a fairy on your shoulder, brush it off."

"Stupid pests." Brax complained trying to get the fairy off his shoulder but it persisted, fluttering about Brax's ear. It buzzed his face and Brax desperately tried to shoo it away. Brax flailed about, wildly waving his hands. "Argh, I can't stand fairies."

"Wait!" Thomas's face grew ashen.

"Now what? What can be worse than being harassed by a fairy?"

Thomas didn't speak, he just pointed straight forward. Out of the brush on the trail ahead popped three dargons. A dargon is a foul creature, it stands three feet high but it has lizard like tail six feet long with a thorn shaped stinger at the end that whips about when it fights. Brown and black, it looks like a large insect, with six short pincers running up and down each side of its body. They were no more than fifty feet away and when they saw Thomas and Brax they gave out an evil hiss. The one in front spat at the boys which landed in front of them smoking and sizzling when it hit the ground. Thomas drew his bow and killed the one in front with a direct shot to its head. Two more dargons jumped out of the weeds from beside them and Brax drew his sword and severing their heads. When the bodies hit the ground black blood oozed out and they twitched and convulsed as if a maniacal puppeteer controlled them. Thomas dropped two others lingering in some brush hitting the ground with a thud when his arrows pierced.

Thomas's heart was pounding and he was breathing hard. It was his first time in combat and he was shocked that he had acted without thinking. He had killed the dargons with no more thought than putting on his shirt in the morning and strangely, Thomas felt very alive. He tingled from the adrenaline rushing through his body.

Brax was panting and huffing, kneeling over at the waist and looking down at the dirt. "Did you see that!" He yelled and then he started laughing.

"Yeah I saw that, we kicked some dargon ass, that's what we did."

"Hells yeah we did. We kicked it, we took its name, and sent the rest running for their mothers." Brax's voice trailed off towards the end of that statement and he grew silent. His mouth dropped and stared across an open field.

"What is it?"

"Run!"

Thomas looked across the field where Brax was staring and a horde of dargons were running towards them, more like slithering but they were very fast.

They both took off as fast as they could run and Brax gained about ten feet on Thomas because he never looked back. Thomas had to look to see how many were there were, there must have been a twenty or thirty and there was no way the two of them could take them all on. They were in pursuit of both of them like the devil on a sinner.

"What do we do!" Brax yelled.

Thomas looked back again and saw that they were getting closer. "Run faster."

"Another great plan!" Yelled Brax.

They ran at break neck speed across the field, not stopping.

"Can they climb trees?" Thomas called out.

"I have no idea."

"I don't think I can keep up this pace much longer." Thomas yelled.

"Me either. I was worn out before we started."

"Me too. I'm starting to cramp up. I'm not going to make it."

"Don't say that, keep running. We can make this."

"We need to make up a tree before they gain on us."

"What good will that do? We don't know if they can climb up after us."

"At least we can fight them off easier. They can't all climb up at once."

"All right, that's the best plan we've got I guess. What tree then?"

"The one straight ahead, it has high branches but we can reach the bottom ones."

Thomas and Brax doubled their speed in a mad dash for a tall tree standing straight in front of them, it was only tree in a clearing and any other day Thomas would have admired how grand it truly was. Brax reached the tree first, and quickly climbed up the first three limbs. Thomas was quickly behind him and swung up the branches like a monkey, his arms were the only thing not tired.

Thomas readied his bow. The first two dargons to reach the tree fell to their deaths but soon a dozen more showed up and Thomas quickly ran out of arrows. The dargons circled around the tree, one of them tried to spit up at them but it fell back in its face and it began to scream from the self-inflicted acid burn. They began to circle around rearing up on their tails and hissing wildly.

"Good news." Thomas said.

"Really! Do tell, what is the good news?" Said Brax looking at him disbelief.

"They can't climb trees." Thomas said laughing.

Brax looked down at them incredulously and nodded. "I guess that is somewhat good news, but you're out of arrows and there are still at least twenty of those nasty little buggers left."

The sun was setting low in the sky and the two sat in the tree through the morning and into the late afternoon. The dargons showed no signs of ending their siege on the tree and two boy's spirits were starting to slowly give away for any hope of getting out of the predicament. They had dropped their bags to climb the tree and now they had no food.

Unseen by Thomas and Brax, a creature about two feet tall sat in another tree not far them, he was red faced with a long nose and pointy ears. His arms were disproportionately long and when he walked his knuckles dragged on the ground. His fists were also large, like two hams hanging from a tree branch. He was a clubber gnome, and he sat waiting to see if the two boys were going to be eaten by the dargons, and if not if not by dargons he was certainly hoping for a shot at making a large feast out of them. Either way it would be a good show, he even brought a few snacks along in anticipation of the event. What clubber gnomes have for snacks is not at all appetizing to humans, and most would want to avert their eyes when a clubber gnome begins any meal. The clubber gnome sat idly, his feet dangling from the limb and swaying back and forth. He hoped the dargons would leave at least a couple of bones for him to gnaw on.

Thomas didn't notice the clubber gnome, his eyes were still intent on the dargons below, twenty-two to be precise. He had nothing better to do but to count them as the afternoon shifted to late evening. Brax named them to pass the time. They looked down at their packs laying at the base of the tree, the dargons had torn them to pieces eating the food, and one of them took off running with the bag of gems.

"That one is Stubby." Brax decided. "And that one over there by the other tree is Victor."

"Victor?"

"Strange name for a dargon."

"Sorry, I'm running out of names."

"That one over there is Bartholomew."

"You have put too much thought into this." Thomas said.

"Sorry, besides being absolutely terrified, I'm really pretty bored." Brax said.

"There's twenty-two."

"Are you sure?"

"Yes, I've counted them five times." Thomas said. "What's that one's name over by the rock?"

"Frederick." Brax nodded knowingly.

"Look over there!!"

"What?"

"It was girl."

"A human girl?"

"Yes I'm almost certain of it."

A girl stepped out of the woods, turned around, and went back into the woods, then came back out. She had long red hair that looked like a spaghetti factory exploded on her head. She was wearing leather pants and on her back was a lute.

"She looks lost." Brax said. "We should call her for help."

"No don't." Thomas stopped him.

"Why not?"

"If the dargons see her she'll be in the same mess we're in."

"Well that's ok I was getting lonely up here with just you to talk with."

"Very funny."

But they didn't have to call the girl, Aurella had noticed them first. She also noticed the twenty something dargons sniffling around at the bottom of the tree. She didn't hesitate, she drew out her lute as if it were a weapon and began playing furiously on it. To Brax and

Thomas's surprise the dargons began to shriek and took off running. Aurella walked up to the tree and looked up at the two young man perched in tree like a couple of birds.

The clubber gnome was stunned that two humans had managed to get out of the problem and he huffed off into a hole in the side of the tree, his knuckles dragging along the thick limb. "No leftovers today." He muttered.

Aurella walked up to the tree and putting her hands on her hips she smiled. "Why are you in the middle of these woods playing with dargons?"

"We weren't exactly playing with them." Thomas said matter of factly. "We killed quite a few of them, that is until we ran out of arrows."

"Why didn't you make more arrows out of some of those branches?"

Brax looked at Thomas, "Yes Thomas why didn't you?"

"Shut up. You didn't think of it either."

"It still doesn't explain why you are out in the middle of this place, these woods are dangerous."

"We're on an adventure." Thomas said.

"Yes. A quest of sorts." Brax piped in.

"A Quest? What sort of quest?" She asked.

"A Quest to make riches, slay dragons, and rescue maidens." Brax said.

"Well this maiden had to save you."

"A mere technicality. We would have been ok." Replied Brax.

"Alright then. I can summon them back with my lute."

"No no, that's ok I don't want to take my chances." Thomas interjected and nudged Brax to keep quiet.

"I'll leave you two boys to continue on your, ahem…cough… quest." She smiled at Thomas who blushed. Aurella turned to go.

"Wait." Thomas exclaimed.

Aurella stopped and turned back around looking straight at Thomas. "Yes." She said blinking her eyes.

"Wait." Thomas said again. "We lost all our food to the dargons. They cleaned our packs and took all our supplies. They didn't leave us with anything."

"So you need more of my assistance?" Aurella's smile became even bigger.

"Yes we need your help." Said Thomas. "I… I can pay you. Don't worry we're not beggars."

"I could be persuaded to help you."

Thomas looked into her eyes, and his heart dropped. He felt it drop down in his chest and he had to catch his breath for a second. She was beautiful and her smile caught him off guard. Her eyes sparkled and twinkled and her hair cascaded to her shoulders. Red flowing hair. He caught himself absently staring into her eyes and in the instant he realized he was in love with her. There was a brief awkward silence and she stared back into his eyes.

"What?" She asked.

Thomas snapped out of his mesmerizing stupor, "We don't need much. A few days' supplies and some fresh water." He managed to stammer out.

"Follow me. I will take you to my father's house."

"That'll be perfect." Thomas said.

"And what is your name adventurer?"

"I'm Thomas, this is Brax. And who are you?"

"Aurella. Get your gear, it won't be long before more dargons start coming back around. That was just a scouting party."

Thomas and Brax picked up what was left of their supplies and quickly followed Aurella. Aurella walked fast and Thomas was surprised he had trouble keeping up with her. She nimbly jumped from rock to fallen log without a problem. They were not on any type of trail and Brax was wondering if she was going to abandon them in the middle of nowhere to rob them.

"Stop it, Thomas." Brax said.

Thomas acted surprised. "Stop what?"

"I see how you're looking at her. It's the same way you looked at Rachael in school."

"That was a long time ago."

"Still the same. You're in love with this girl. And she's fix'n to rob us in the middle of the woods and leave us for dead."

"We don't have anything for her to steal, brainchild."

"I still have my sword."

"I don't think she's going to do that after saving us."

"You don't know that. You barely know this girl and you're falling in love with her. Stop it, we have plans. We're going places and see the world remember."

"I'm not falling in love."

"Yes you are.I can see it in your eyes."

"I'm ok. Stop worrying. We'll still go on adventures."

"I'm just saying. I'd rather see us become pirates than have you falling in love again. You were a mess the entire fourth grade."

The came into a clearing and Aurella put her hands into the air, spinning around on her toes. "We're here." She proudly proclaimed.

"We're where?" Asked Thomas.

"I told you. She's taking us to the middle of nowhere and leaving as to the wolves."

"This is my father's house."

In the middle of the clearing was a small mound of earth, and for the first time Thomas realized that there was a chimney coming out of the ground in the middle, and a light wispy trail of smoke was coming out. There were purple and yellow wildflowers all about the clearing and there was the smell of hickory wood burning in the air.

"Come in. You can meet my father." She said.

Aurella's father, Skylan Mac Brenner was a giant of a man with long braided red beard that reached down to his bellybutton. Thomas was tall, but this man before him was a foot taller. His massive hands could grip a broad axe like a child's toy. He had a massive nose and broad face, and all Thomas could think was that Aurella certainly didn't get her beauty from her father.

"Who are you?" He glared down at Thomas.

"Thomas." Thomas stammered.

Brax didn't say anything out of fear. Skylan didn't say a word, he just eyed Thomas up and down as if Thomas was facing inspection.

"I'm Thomas Kray."

"Captain Kray's son?"

"Yes sir."

"Captain Holden Kray, hero of the second battle of Mayhem Ridge?"

For a second Thomas wondered if he was a friend or an enemy of his father, but he placed one foot forward and decided to hold fast to his conviction.

"Lord Holden Kray is my father." He said with assurance.

Skylan grabbed Thomas like a rag doll, picked him up and hugged him. "Come in boy, any son of Holden Kray is welcome here. How is your father, boy?"

When Skylan let go of his massive bear hug, Thomas let out the bad news. "He's passed on sir, defending the citadel."

"That's a hard blow to hear about, son. I fought beside him on that cursed ridge, I'll never forget it. A great man he was."

Thomas breathed a sigh of relief.

"Never a greater man than your father. If you're half of him, you'll be great as well."

"I'll try to live up to him."

"You're Skylan Mac Brennan?"

"Aye lad."

"My father spoke well of you as well."

"Well then, come in. I've got a pot full of sausage, cabbages, and potatoes, and an old whiskey. You're more than welcome in my house."

"Thank you, sir."

"No need to call me sir, I worked for a living son."

"Yes mister Mac Brennan."

"My father likes to be called Big Sarge." Aurella chimed in.

"A bit late in the year to be travelling. In a few more months' winter will be setting in. Where you headed to?"

"Nowhere in particular mister Skylan. Pirates, thieves, or soldiers…all seem a mighty fine life for us." Thomas said. "We just haven't decided yet. We're just look'in to be steered in the right direction I reckon."

When Skylan laughed his belly shook and beard wiggled. "I want you to do a favor for me, that is if you're up to it."

"A quest?" Brax asked.

"Of sorts. There's an island far off the coast of the Four Corners. Trilliane is its name. It's small, not very settled except for some hardy people and hardier sheep. Aurella has an aunt that lives there."

"Seeing someone's aunt at Trilliane ain't much of quest." Brax said.

"Hold on, I'm not finished. I want you take Aurella there. Take her across the sea, it's no longer safe here and I'm too old to make the journey."

"Still not much of a quest."

"Shut up Brax."

"No worries. I've gold set aside for her, she'll pay her own way, I just want to make sure she gets there. Her brother was supposed to take her, but he went hunting ten days ago and hasn't returned. I fear worst for him."

"We'll do it." Thomas said.

"We will?" Proclaimed Brax reluctantly.

"Yes, we will gladly take her."

It was late night, darkness set in over the underground house and ate their dinner like it was their last.

Chapter 4

Melfling

Behold, I come as a thief. Blessed is he that watcheth, and keepeth his garments,Lest he walk naked, and they see his shame

- Revelation 16

Moshki went to the bar and ordered another drink. The only problem was that when the words came out of his mouth to speak to the bartender, he said "Porba shlapy peeva." The bartender just looked at him disdainfully.

"Stupid melfling." The bartender mumbled.

Often when Moshki was a little tipsy, he would slip into his native tongue. Shrugging off the evil eye the bartender was giving, Moshki dug deep into the pocket of his multicolored vest and pulled out a coin. "Sorry, another bottle of ale, please." Moshki said as he reached up, hiccupped and stood on his tiptoes to slide a single silver piece over to the burly, unshaven man tending the bar. The bartender did not give him any change, but Moshki didn't care, he was a heavy tipper anyway, and fairly wealthy.

Moshki was wealthy because he was one of the most successful thieves in town, in fact he was vice-chairman of the local Thieves' Guild which was headquartered thirty feet below the Drunken Dragon Inn which was only accessible by an intricate maze of ancient drain pipes. Moshki was rather peculiar for a melfling because he did not like getting dirty at all, when he would go to the monthly thieves meeting he would don thick wader-boots and an overcoat so as not to get his clothes or himself soiled, although the drainage pipes were no longer used, it was covered in thick muck. And cleaning the muck out of his fine furry body was burdensome.

Moshki liked his clothes, and he could afford purchasing the very finest available. He had them tailor made at the most expensive place in the city and his tastes did not stop there, he also rented a large, elaborate flat on the third floor of the Drunken Dragon Inn. Large only in Melfling terms, though, because a human could barely stick their fat heads through the entrance of his apartment. The third floor of the inn was rented to those who were of smaller stature; gnomes and dwarves could also be seen bustling through the hallways. Most humans would eye him suspiciously, and Moshki was never sure if it was because he looked like a three-foot tall mouse, or that they suspected him of being a thief. He often worried about the latter because he did live lavishly and he did not hold a job. This point was often brought up when he would hang out in the bar but he would reply that a wealthy relative had left him the money. Other members of the Thieves' Guild held steady, or at least part-time jobs for cover, but Moshki really could not stand to get up that early just for work, and there was little opportunity for someone so small.

The only real difficulty that Moshki had was that stealing anything large would weigh him down to the point he couldn't move, he was agile and clever but not very strong. So he had to either steal light expensive things or make several trips. And since the bartender liked to keep his change, he had to work often just in thieving. If he didn't leave the tip Moshki was afraid he would get no ale at all, and that would be even sadder. So Moshki's ears and nose pricked up when he saw the men from the Wizard's federation walk in and sat down in a dark corner. Moshki knew that they would have the paper money that they favored. It was difficult to exchange, but worth the trouble and certainly light enough for his little stature.

Slipping off of the barstool, Moshki walked to the back of the bar where it was dark at any time of day, and put on his cloak. Moshki's cloak was special in that when he wore it and pulled the hood all the way over his pointy ears, he was virtually invisible. It wasn't an invisibility cloak, Moshki couldn't that amount of magic, but it was camouflaged for such urban endeavors like a dimly lit tavern. Moshki actually did inherit the cloak from his uncle Sasha, who received it from a great enchantress that gave it to him for saving her live. Actually Sasha probably stole it too, but he would always tell a grand story about saving the enchantress.

Being almost invisible could cause problems for Moshki because some clumsy human could step on him, so he had to take care in walking close to the walls. He inched his way to the four men sitting in the corner. He flexed his fingers nimbly as he hugged the wall, the man closest to him was a young human who seemed an easy mark. He deftly stuck his paw into the young man's robes and pulled out a few coins, one at a time. It was gold! What luck Moshki cried out in his own mind. He pulled out a scroll, a vial full of a glowing liquid, and a pocketknife. I have enough pocketknives to open my own store, Moshki thought to himself, which was not an entirely bad idea. He could call it Moshki's pocket watch and knife Shoppe; it could be a great side business from thieving. He thrust his greedy paw in one more time and retrieved a roll of federation paper money, he chuckled silently and thought how easy it was

Moshki slid back along the wall away from the four men as he stealthily made his way towards them. Moving to the back of the room before taking his cloak off so as not to alarm anyone with a suddenly appearing melfling. He went back to the bar and while ordering another beer he spotted the most beautiful melfling girl he had ever seen in his life. Humans could not possibly tell one melfling from the next but to melflings, the difference was all to apparent. Licking his paws, Moshki slicked back the hair on his head and behind his ears then sidled over to the girl who had just sat down by herself at a table.

Smiling coyly to her, he said, "Pardon me madam, I have not seen you in this town before, and there are very few melflings here, and I am in dire need of true melfling fellowship. Might ask for your name?"

"My name is Katrina." She giggled.

Moshki's ears pricked up, "Ahh, Katrina, what a beautiful name. Are you here for a visit, or are you just passing through this wonderful outpost?"

"I came here to meet someone; they should be here any minute." She replied.

"You smell ravishing Katrina, like the scent of cheese and …" Moshki paused a moment. "Herring. Very delightful."

The melfling girl giggled once more. "Do you have the time?" She asked.

What luck, Moshki thought, two melfling women. "Why yes my dear, it's a quarter to ten." He said, stylishly pulling out his gold watch with much flair.

That moment became Moshki's downfall. A man sitting at another table grabbed Moshki's wrist to look at the watch. "Where did you get this?" He shouted.

The man wasn't very big but to Moshki he seemed like a giant. He looked angry and agitated.

"My dear sir, I take offense to your implication. This watch was given to me by my great grandfather on his deathbed, not moments before his passing." Moshki replied with great indignation and wrenching his wrist from the man's grasp. "You, sir, should take care to whom you accuse, I have many connections in this town." Moshki said loudly in an attempt to draw attention and embarrass his accuser.

A shadow of doubt briefly fell over the man's face but he grabbed the watch from Moshki's paw and opened it. "From your great grandfather says you, well the inscription reads to Big Jed your loving wife, always."

"Indeed sir, my grandfather Big Jed." Said Moshki not backing down.

"I'm Big Jed!" The gruff man shouted.

By now a small crowd had formed around them and there was no easy escape for Moshki. The melfling girl was now looking at him with crossed arms and one raised eyebrow. Katrina's friend joined her, and it was not another female melfling but Pasha, a melfling Moshki recognized from the Thieves' Guild.

Moshki looked towards Pasha with a facial expression that pleaded for help, hoping that he would create some sort of diversion that would aide in Moshki's escape. He could count on Pasha he thought. He was my buddy, my guild chum. That's what being in the Thieves' Guild was all about, the comradery and having one another's back.

Pasha raised a shaking fist and shouted, "It's melflings like you that give us a bad name!"

"Kick his arse Big Jed!" someone else shouted.

"Meep." Was all that came out of Moshki's mouth.

Big Jed grabbed him by his silk vest and punched him square in the nose, sending him with force through the swinging doors of the Drunken Dragon Inn. Moshki fell on his rear and landed on the dirt ground of dirt street in front of the Inn. He sat for a second sitting and holding his nose with stunned disbelief but realized this was not the moment for dilly-dallying. He got up with a shot and darted underneath the building next door to the Drunken Dragon.

The crowd moved outside and several shouted in unison, "Get him! Get him!"

But luckily they were too late, Moshki was already underneath the building and across the other side hiding under different one. The clumsy humans were still clamoring under the last building. With all of Moshki's might he ran across the street, to the sewer system.

"There he is!" he heard someone shout.

But he made it, he was safely in the sewer, no human, except for a child could fit through the entrance to the sewers but the stench was unbearable for Moshki. The sewer led outside of town, all he had to do was follow the flow of water. An hour later he was out of the sewer and he chanced a peak at the town. The commotion had died down, so he made his way to the street. He began walking slowly at first but then picked up his pace, he looked disdainfully back one more time to the town he called home, he would miss it he thought but mostly he would miss his money that he had amassed. The sun died down, and Moshki realized that he could not run farther, the pain in his side burned like a sharp knife… he was no longer the melfling of his youth. He slowed to a halt and collapsed in the ditch beside the road, crawling the rest of the way to a growth of reeds to hide from any passerby's.

The melfling hunt soon turned to apathy, and people slowly turned back to their homes around midnight. The town people quickly lost interest in Moshki, Big Jed had his watch back and no real harm was done. Pasha and the melfling girl Katrina quickly ran away so as not to be mistaken for the recently run out of town rogue. Moshki narrowly missed a good tar and feathering, which would have been a pretty bad ordeal to get out of his fur.

Moshki's nose twitched as the morning sun lit upon his face. With a paw he brushed a whisker and one eye barely came open, it was around ten o'clock in the morning he thought to himself, much too early for a civilized rogue to be getting up this early. He arched his back painfully realizing that the ground was not at all comfortable.

The memories of the night before drifted back to him with great alarm, 'by the gods, I am destitute', he thought himself. He checked his pockets, gone was the pocket watch from one 'Big Jed', but he did have the money from the kind gentleman of the wizard federation, some coins and the strange vial that gave off an unearthly glow. He examined the pocket knife for the first time and considered it to be of some use. By all wonders, he still had on his possession his traveling pipe, it was small and fit nicely in his little hands. Engraved on the side were melfling runes, that many considered to be some sort of ancient spell of warding, some magical incantation but in fact were simply said if found, please return to one Moshki of 13544 Cross Falls, room 24 of the Drunken Dragon Inn. If one looked closely, they could see that the previous owners name and address were carefully scratched off.

Pulling out a bit of tobacco and stuffing it into his pipe, Moshki lit the loose fit tobacco, drawing deep upon it. It was his favorite apple blend. He sat down cross legged in the middle of the road, wondering which direction he should go. Maybe it was good thing he was on his way from Cross Falls, he had become pretty complacent in that little village and it was due time he moved on to better places and richer pickings. He smelled himself, and it was bad, when you can smell yourself you know it's bad.

He stood up examining all directions, east and west, north and south with equal puzzlement. "Fruzzle!" the ancient melfling curse escaped from his lips as a wisp of smoke floated in the air. "Which way is better?"

The fates should decide he thought, he pulled the telling bones from his breeches and pocket and tossed them on the road. West, they told him. That's odd indeed, he thought to himself. "I've never been west before, should be interesting." He said aloud as if talking to the bones themselves. "Need to find someone to burgle before too long though, else I'll get hungry, besides I need new clothes. These smell like the depths of the sewer."

Moshki started trotting west, thinking of things that were better than his current plight. Such as, breakfast at the Drunken Dragon Inn, his gold, other people's gold and being in the arms of that cute melfling girl he met the night before…what was her name he wondered. "Katrina." He goofily said aloud, and a smile beamed across is whiskered face.

Moshki walked along the road, happily whistling a tune. One thing he learned in life was never let bump in the road drag you down. Keep on going he always told himself. What lies ahead maybe better than what you just lost. Moshki passed an old man carrying a bundle of sticks on his back. He was old. He had dark and leathery skin with a beard so white it looked like a puff of snow clinging to his chin. He nodded at Moshki silently and went on his way. For a short moment Moshki turned to look at him, realizing he knew him from somewhere from someplace. He wore a dark gray turban upon his head. Moshki was puzzled. He knew for sure he recognized him. He stopped to watch him go and as he passed from sight it hit Moshki who he was.

He was Death. What was Death doing so far out in the middle of nowhere? Moshki put the thought aside, just glad that death had passed him by with no more than a just a nod. He knew who he was not because he had seen him before. Moshki never had a brush with death, he liked to keep things safe. Oh sure, he was a thief, and a darn good one. But he was a safe thief. Nothing risky, no leaping from or scaling tall buildings. He didn't elude guards. Pickpocketing was simple and efficient. No, he knew Death from the paintings depicting him. Curious.

"My luck is changing. Death passed me be by with no more than a nod, and now I've found this wonderful clear spring to bathe in."

Moshki jumped in the water with a great splash. Moshki relished in scrubbing the sewer sludge off his body and began whistling. Pondering for a moment, Moshki wondered what was doing walking that way, there was something bad going to happen. The melfling now cleaned and feeling better about himself, decided to take a short cut through the fields. He sat on a rock, to sit in the cool autumn sun and dry himself off. A spot of cheese would be nice. That's when the ground below him, for no apparent reason began to collapse. Moshki fell a good ten feet, landing with a thud and the dust that had gathered for hundreds of years billowed up around him.

He was in a dark room, and his night vision kicked in. "I hope there's food about this place." He muttered. He closed his left eye and spied around the room, it was a habit, not really anything productive. There was a box of crackers in the corner, hundreds of years old or not. He was going to eat those crackers. He was famished. He opened the tin like a fiend and began stuffing his face. He wondered if he was getting out of this mess, when upon the wall he saw something even better than crackers. Bottles of rum and whisky.

Chapter 5

Bard

Cry "havoc!" and let loose the dogs of war, that this foul deed shall smell above the earth. With carrion men, groaning for burial.

-William Shakespeare

Opening the door just a crack, Aurella peeked into the living room where Thomas and Braxton lay on the floor before a dying fire on top of a thick fur rug. For the past two days that those boys had come to stay in their house she could not keep her mind off of Thomas, he was tall and handsome and a certain awkwardness that made him charming. She felt that she had been way too bold on their first meeting and now felt a little ashamed. But she knew that Thomas held some kind of feeling for her, she caught him staring at her more than once and then shyly look away. But Aurella felt herself falling in love. She was only sixteen years old; she told herself before that she would never fall in love so young like her mother had done years before.

Aurella made an oath, years before, underneath the seven stars, that the man who would be her true love would give her a sign. The sign was simple in itself; the man must give her posies underneath an elm tree. That was it, no roses, they were pretentious, no dandelions, only a fool would give those and an elm tree? Why not, those were her rules and part of the oath that she made.

Thomas stirred a little on the floor and for a second she swore that he looked up at her. She burst open the door and with a loud voice said, "Time to get up lazy bones."

Braxton uttered some unintelligible words and rolled over but Thomas looked up into her eyes. She couldn't help smiling at him.

"I will make us some breakfast, up with you and go wash. Especially you Braxton Aleman, you smell like a donkey."

Braxton uttered more words under his breath and stumbled to the washbasin, splashing cold water on his face to clear his sleepy eyes.

Later on that day Thomas lay in the cool of a grove of trees on the side of a hill, twirling a blade of grass about with his tongue as he sucked on the sweet nectar of the end. It was that time of year when the weather could not decide whether to be cold or hot. Thomas was learning much from Skylan, Aurella's father. He was patient and kind to them, nothing like the stories he heard of his father's teacher. Holden Kray told him about his training to become a soldier and the brutalities he endured, but Skylan was nothing like that, he taught them the ways of nature and survival with care.

Thomas took a small sip of the cayenne water that Aurella made to wake himself. It was the drink of ranger's. So Skylan said, it will revive you, heal you and give you the heat for battle. The creeds that Skylan drilled into their memories came into Thomas's thoughts, a ranger always uses the advantage of stealth, a ranger never leaves a comrade behind, a ranger sticks to the code.

As he slipped into sleepiness, more thoughts came rushing into his head and the picture of his father lying on the death cart that brought him home, the lightning revealing his pale, unmoving death face. It was not the way he wanted to remember his dad and tried to close out the memory and fight back the tears and bitterness. He tried to remember a happier time, he recalled the day when they moved into the old stone farm house, the land held five hundred apple trees, Thomas counted them all, and in the spring, the white blossoms covered the ground like snow on a winters day. And there walking through Thomas's daydream with blossoms swirling about her as if she commanded them was Aurella.

Thomas stood up and shook the feelings for her from his heart. He felt guilty, so soon after his parent's death he was falling in love with her. The last thing he needed was a girl in his life; she would slow him down and try to make settle him down.

He took another sip of the cayenne water and as burned going down he spotted a small bunch of posies growing amongst a rocky outcropping.

"No you're not, Thomas." Braxton broke the dreamlike revelry Thomas was in, with the shattering of his voice.

"Yes I am." Thomas said with the utmost determination.

"You can't Tom, you give those flowers to her we'll ne'er have adventures. You'll settle down and pop out li'l Thomas's and li'l Aurella's and she'll be griping at you cause you tracked mud in da house."

"Shut up Braxton!"

"Thomas I'm a telling ya, you give her those you'll get married and you'll ne'er slay an ogre, ne'er kill a dragon and ne'er see a gold coin cause she's gonna hide any that ya bring home."

"I don't care Braxton, I don't want to be alone the rest of my days, and I can't explain it, I was feeling the same way you are now, but as soon as I saw them posies it changed everything in my life."

Thomas ran from Braxton, he couldn't understand himself but he knew at that moment, the very second he laid eyes on the posies growing where no posies should be growing, in between a bunch of rocks, all doubt was removed and he had to give them to Aurella, it was if he was driven to it.

Sitting on the front door of their house, Aurella strummed her small six stringed lute with a haunting melody. Thomas stopped and stared; it was if he could see the song drifting through the air. He almost heeded Braxtons' words and threw the flowers on the ground but he picked them back up and continued down the hill.

"These are for you." He stammered, thrusting out the flowers to Aurella.

"No." She cried almost shouting.

"Huh?" Thomas was crestfallen. He thought for sure that she would fall in love with him the moment he gave her the flowers. Posies, of all things, he should have known better and should have looked for something special like roses.

But Aurella grabbed him and pulled him underneath a huge elm tree not ten feet away from where they were standing. The tree, growing in their front yard, was older than all of them combined, majestic and true.

"Give them to me here." She almost demanded.

"What, huh?" Were all the words he could manage to get out of his mouth.

"It's part of the prophecy, you have to give me the flowers underneath an elm tree, this elm tree."

"What prophecy?" Thomas gave up all reasoning at that point and was sure that reasoning would never enter into their relationship from that moment forward.

He gave her the posies, underneath the largest, stateliest elm Thomas had ever seen and Aurella threw her arms around him and Thomas kissed her. A strong passionate kiss, that made her weak and made him strong. At that time everything stood still, there was no danger, no monsters taking over the land and no worries. The brown and purple leaves hung in midair as they were falling to the ground, the earth stopped spinning and the sun came down just a little closer, just to be with them.

Later that evening they gathered around the dinner table for a grand feast of roast chickens and fresh pears with nuts. This day Thomas joined Aurella in the kitchen to help her with preparing the food, cutting the fresh herbs and talking all the while. Aurella told him how that she lost her own mother only last year after she caught the fever. She told him of her brother, Jacob, who was on a long hunting trip but was due back very soon but she was worried. Thomas told her of his family and the farm he grew up on, and how he lost his mother and that everything had been destroyed.

"Aren't you sad?" She asked him.

"I don't know." He said. "It's not really sadness, I feel cold inside, as if someone has taken all the warmth from body."

"I still grow sad whenever I think of my mother, I miss her every day."

"What do you to help that?"

"I don't." She said. "I don't want to stop missing her, or forget her. There's an old stone bridge down by a creek, not far from here. I go there sometimes after picking flowers, and I cast the petals into the water. The memories of her come back to me and I sing her favorite song."

"My mother practiced magic, she would sprinkle tobacco around our house to ward off evil spirits and she tied knots to bring us good fortune, but that was the extent of her magic. I've heard of magicians that can conjure up demons and shoot fire." Thomas said.

"Your mother sounds wonderful, don't forget her." Aurella said.

"The towns people told rumors that my mother cast a love spell upon my father, because there was no explanation that a noble man like he was, could fall in love with a woman in the practice. I don't believe it though, love spells or potions never last that long. He loved her till the day he died."

"I can't wait for you to meet my brother Jacob; you are so much alike." Aurella said.

"Really, what's he like?"

"He's tall, handsome and quiet like you are, only he's a little impatient like Braxton is. He's the same age as you are and he's doing a very ill attempt at growing a beard, it's coming in all scraggly but he wants to look older and tougher than he is."

"I can't wait to meet him. You really think I'm handsome?" He asked.

Aurella didn't answer him; she just looked into his eyes silently.

"You know, I've seen you before, last year as matter of fact" Said Thomas. "It was at midfest in Greystone, you and your parents were there. Brax and I were getting tipsy drinking hard cider. I noticed you, you were standing by the bonfire in the night, and there were little children gathered around you, listening to you play."

"And I've seen you before, Sir Thomas. We were mere toddlers, my father went to visit your father at your farm and you were climbing an apple tree not paying a bit of attention a to a little girl hiding behind her daddy's leg." She splashed some water on him playfully and Thomas looked down shyly not knowing what to say.

That evening Thomas lay on the living room floor, his eyes wide open, staring sleeplessly at the rocky ceiling where a few roots poked down into the underground dwelling. He wondered if Aurella was doing the same. The fire warmed his body and he wanted to know if this was love. It must be he thought... he was excited, nervous, his heart was pounding through his chest whenever Aurella was near him and he couldn't stop thinking of her. He rolled over and thought of a poem about her, he wished he knew how to write them down.

Thinking of you keeps me awake.

Dreaming of you keeps me asleep.

Being with you keeps me alive.

He hoped he could remember and someday write the words down. When sleep came to Thomas, it came so hard that he did not hear the front door open. The tall shadowy figure silently entered the house and dropped a bag on the kitchen table. He sat down at the table and pulled off his muddy moccasins. Thomas usually woke to the sound of a house mouse, but it didn't matter to Brax, who always slept like a bear in midwinter and never had a moment's trouble falling asleep… even if an avalanche crashed down around him or a volcano erupted beside him. The real surprise came for Jacob who found a two strange young men sleeping in his living room. One asleep curled up in front of the fire the other on a chair his head drooped to one side and drool dripping from his mouth.

Drawing his long hunting knife from its leather sheath, he didn't take any chances. Pouncing on the curled up ball on the floor, which in this case was Thomas, Jacob put the blade to his throat and pinned his arms down with his knees.

"Answer who you are or I'll slit you a new smile!" Jacob demanded.

Thomas, so stunned he didn't even put up a fight, answered, "I'm Thomas, Thomas Kray of Greystone." He barely managed to get the words out through sudden fear and the inability to move.

Brax rolled over to his right, mumbled, snorted but still slept soundly.

"What in the Four Corners are you doing in my house and where is the rest of my family?"

Realizing who his assailant was Thomas began explaining. "Jacob, your father and sister took us into your household, my parents were killed our town was destroyed by strange men from the east."

"Prove it!"

"How else would I know your name"? Jacob relaxed but didn't let his guard down. Thomas sat up, getting a bit irritated and carefully slid the knife away from his throat.

"Jacob!" Aurella cried out. "Put that knife down and leave Thomas alone! That's a fine way to treat our guests, assaulting them in the middle of the night and nearly killing them."

"I'm sorry." Said Jacob, extending his hand to help Thomas up off the floor. "I didn't know who you were, thought maybe you were thieves."

"Thieves!" Aurella yelled "Thieves don't come in, leave everything untouched and fall asleep on the floor." Aurella took her stance again, the brazen stance with her hands on her hips and her hair falling down to her waist.

Realizing that she was clad only in her nightie and Thomas was gazing wide eyed at her, she crossed her arms to cover herself and turned around. She slapped Jacob in the back of the head, "Off to bed with ye, Jacob Ravensong." She ordered, and then returned to her room.

Jacob looked at Thomas and shrugged, "Sorry." He said and went to his own room.

Thomas grimaced, still feeling the knife's edge at his throat, "It's ok, nothing really."

Brax rolled over to his left, mumbled, snorted and continued to sleep.

The next morning was eventful and festive. Skylan and Aurella were both relieved and elated that Jacob came home at last after a weeklong hunting trip. They were disappointed to discover he was unable to bring home any fresh meat.

"The land is barren, father." Jacob explained. "All the wild game has moved elsewhere. I think the dargons are pushing their way south and in this direction. Not only has all the game left, so have all the other animals, the eagles, the fish, I didn't even see a wildcat. I saw one rambler, eating ants down by the stream and that was all, and no human can stomach those."

"Thomas and I saw a lone dargon scout three days ago." Brax interjected. "He made off with our bag full of all the money we had and our provisions."

"I killed a dargon yesterday." Jacob said excitedly. "It had a bag in his mouth!"

Thomas and Brax shot each other a look of joy. They had their money back!

"There was no money in it." Said Jacob.

"What about the gems? There were diamonds, sapphires and an even an emerald in that bag." Said Thomas.

"Yes, the gems are in there."

"What about the beef jerky?" asked Brax.

Aurella gave Braxton a look of incredulity; she couldn't believe after losing thousands of gold, he was worried about food.

"No beef jerky but there was this book." Jacob said, flipping it over in his hands and then handing it to Thomas.

All the wind fell out of Thomas, his sudden joy turned again. Thomas looked the book over, not much worse for wear after being in a dargons' mouth for three days. He recognized his father's name in the lower right hand corner in gold leaf, putting it in the pocket of his leather tunic.

"I'm sorry Thomas, this was all that was left."

"Hold on to the book lad." Said Skylan. "Your father saw fit to hold on to it, so should you. It won't make you rich but it may prove to be of other values someday."

"What are we going to do father?" Asked Aurella. "From what Jacob says, the whole dargon horde may be coming this way soon."

"Aye, right you are. We have to move and now. It's not going to be safe here any longer. We pack our things today and I want you to head south to safety, go to Korinth, it is a port city on the bay, the road lead straight to it. I'm going north to Mission Keep to warn the army."

"But father…" Aurella cried.

"No buts, Aurella. No arguments. I'll be ok and I trust in the four of you, stick together and then you'll be safe."

Skylan took a bag of coins from his side and pushed them into Aurella's' hands. "Take this, head to Korinth like a said and book passage to Trilliaine. I'll join as soon as I can."

The next morning the travelers said their goodbyes, Skylan kissed Aurella on the forehead and gave Jacob a hearty hug. Thomas and Brax gave many thanks to him for his generosity.

Skylan leaned close and spoke into Thomas' ear, "Remember get to the Isle of Trilliaine, no matter what else you do… keep my daughter safe."

"Yes sir." He replied, the burden of realization suddenly hit Thomas, squarely in the jaw. Skylan was entrusting him with Aurella's life.

"Your father and I were at Trilliaine many ages ago, when we were not much older than you are now. There's no place safer than all the four corners."

Thomas was a little taken a back, his father had never mentioned being in Trilliane.

Skylan turned, cutting through the north end of the Nightsbridge forest. His grey beard wagging as he carefully plodded his way with his walking stick. Aurella watched him until he disappeared on the horizon. She couldn't take it anymore and the tears flowed down her cheeks like small pearls. She knew in her heart she would never see him again.

They kept to east side of the forest, and off the trails so as not to be seen by dargon scouts. The small company, not much more than children, began their journey with trepidation. They all feared the worse could happen, Jacob didn't want to leave the valley he called home, but he couldn't stay either. Jacob had packed his knapsack as light as possible; he brought jerked meat, a bedroll and his fur-lined cloak for the coming winter. He carried every weapon he owned, a short sword, his long bow, and throwing knives lined the inside of his jacket. For protection, underneath his tunic he wore the ring mail that belonged to his father, the silver chains were visible in folds around his neck.

Aurella on the other hand, thought her brother looked ridiculous. She packed much lighter but it was as much as she could to carry. Her bag held an ample supply of sun dried nuts and berries mixed together, the mere thought of eating jerky made her stomach retch. More importantly, she brought all of her healing vials, small bottles of a potent green liquid that cured anything but death. She packed every bit of healing potion she ever brewed and if worse came to worse she could make more. It was a simple mixture of herbs that grew in the fields, then fermented. It could get you equally drunk if you drank just a small amount but it wasn't recommended to drink it if you weren't sick or wounded. On her back she carried her lute, a beautifully crafted six-string piece with magical markings written along the sides and in her pocket she carried her flute. Both instruments were older than anyone knew and was passed down through her family.

Aurella's magic was in her music, she never carried weapons, she had no use or need for them. She could play her songs and simply make the enemy fall asleep. With her flute she could conjure up the wind and blow them away like the leaves on a fall day. She had the power of nature at her beckoning with a song.

Aurella brought her fur cloak as well but the cold seldom bothered her, her gauzy white robes were nearly see through and Thomas watched her as she trotted out in front of them, leading the way. He secretly admired the shape of her body her bare smooth lets, her sandals laced up to her knees. Her red hair cascading down her back.

Aurella glanced back at Thomas and smiled, his heart soared and he smiled back. He didn't know why he was still so insecure, after all she had thrown herself into his arms only yesterday and they kissed so passionately. Jacob saw them shooting their eyes at each other and he gave Thomas a protective warning grimace. Thomas took the hint and stopped staring at Aurella. Jacob was overly protective of his little sister and it was a source of some irritation for Aurella.

Borgman spied the land before him through a small brass telescope. They were delayed several days by that incompetent mage on lend from the Dark Order of the Wolf. Ulysses lost the magic potion to find the boy and the key. Ulysses ranted about being pick pocketed and it not being his fault, it did not matter to Borgman but he knew better than do anything about it. He had no desire to awake in the morning as a eunuch, the legendary and purported curse handed down by the Dark of Order of Mages. No Borgman bit his tongue and scanned the land of last known whereabouts that the divining potion pointed to on the map, a place on the eastern edge of Nightsbridge forest, just north of the lake of the dead.

Ten men stood on horseback overlooking the forested hills. Their purple banners unfurled in the wind, the horses stamped their feet in restless anticipation of battle. The men rejoined at the crossroads after splitting up to search for Thomas. They were the Brothers of the Hammer, the brutish arm of the Wizard Federation. They were politicos and Odin Harbinger, as minister of defense, was in charge of the ten. The brothers of the Hammer would slit each other's throats in a second, if they thought it would gain them favor, advancement or a good laugh. All were sent to find the key. The key, as The Prince explained it to him, was a book, only a book. Damn The Prince, thought Odin, sent at his age to find a book. That was his mission. The contents of the book were unclear to him, it didn't matter, he would get the book and get it to The Prince. The Prince intimated to him that the book, if read, caused dissent and rebellion. There was only one copy of it left in all of Four Corners, all others were destroyed, and it was in the possession of Holden Kray who met an unfortunate death in the defense of the Citadel, an outpost in the north. Some idiot passed the book on to his son, Thomas. Odin remembered that idiot well, a Captain Arturas, it took forever to get the information from him and Borgman had a knack for it. Borgman wanted slit his throat afterward like a pig but spared his life.

The Prince was the head of all three branches, the Wizard Federation, the Dark Order of the Mages, and the Brothers of the Hammer. Odin held a strong distrust of magic users despite that his leader was a wizard, come to think of it though Odin distrusted everyone. He watched on as Dag and Borgman whispered into each other's ears like a couple of schoolgirls, conspiring against him he was sure. Odin was old but certainly no fool. Odin knew he had to watch his back the rest of this trip. The triumvirate was locked in a constant battle of control of the Four Corners. They existed in a constant rock, paper, scissors battle and at current it was a man who came from the Wizard Federation House that led the three others. The hammer was vying once more to regain control and crush the Wizard Federation and Borgman was going to what he could to get there.

"There!" said Umar, whose eyes were as sharp as an eagles with the aid of a telescope. "Underneath that large elm, I can see a chimney poking out of the ground."

Borgman was about to say that Umar was in insane, but as he gazed through his telescope he could make out the pile of rocks as a chimney as well.

Harbinger raised his fist in the air and motioned the men forward wordlessly, their armor glistening in the setting sun, the banner of the dragon flapping in the wind they took off down the hill at full speed. Ulysses strode on horseback in the rear, behind the banner carrier. Ulysses knew he was not part of the team, but was glad to be getting the experience and was rather enjoying firsthand the bloodshed and torture.

The underground house was abandoned; the door was left open rocking in the wind. Umar quickly picked up on the signs of hasty withdrawal from the small home, a rather clever design he thought to himself. The cupboards left open, foodstuffs on the ground and the lack of clothing left. It didn't stop them from upturning every piece of furniture, ripping apart the beds and destroying every knickknack. The key needed to be found.

Borgman realized the search was exhausted. "Burn it!" ordered Borgman. "Burn it to the ground."

"But the house is already to the ground." Interjected Ulysses rather flatly.

Borgman bit his tongue once more, daring not to say anything that might offend Ulysses lest he wake up without his testicles in the morning.

The men had some difficulty getting the rock built underground house on fire until Ulysses began casting a spell. Conjuring up a ball of fire while in a mesmeric state, he sent the fireball rolling through the front door like a small child playing with a toy ball. The house burst into flames, fire poured the front door and then up through the ground scorching the grass that grew on top.

"I've spotted their tracks, lord defense minister." Umar reported to Odin Harbinger. "One set barely visible goes in the direction of Mission Keep, four others head south."

"Five people, two directions?" questioned Odin. "Which way is the boy heading?"

"Going south, to be sure lord." Answered Umar. "The boy lacks the skill to hide his tracks so well as the one heading towards Mission Keep, I only found it with difficulty. The ones heading south are smaller, and one is probably a girl."

"He's enlisting the aid of others." Said Borgman who had joined the conversation between Umar and Odin. "Umar, this boy may be more resourceful then I suspected."

"We ride!" Declared Odin, with his armored fist raised in the air once more.

"I need to rest, sir." Ulysses said meekly. "That spell took too much out of me. I need to sit a while underneath this elm tree and regain my strength."

"No time for rest, boy. You can rest on your horse, good god son have a sense of urgency about you."

Ulysses rose to his feet but quickly passed out on the ground.

"Pick him up and strap him to his horse." Ordered Odin.

The men were hesitant, fearing the curse.

"Do it, the eunuch curse is a myth." But Odin thought for a second. "Make sure he is comfortable, put his blanket underneath or something."

Passing the lake of the dead late at night made Brax uneasy, he swore he could see the spirits of ogres and men rising up out of the depths of the misty lake, raising arms to do battle once more for the control of the Four Corners. The moon was a sliver on the horizon and Brax reasoned that his eyes were playing tricks on his mind.

"Want a cool drink of lake water, Brax?" Aurella jibed.

Brax shot back an evil glance.

"Don't drink the water, Brax!" Jacob warned. "The water is cursed."

"So I've been told." Brax said.

They walked on late into the evening, the moon rising illuminating the eerie forest. The air gripping them to their bones and Thomas smelled the first hint of winter in the cold misty evening. Jacob felt the chill air as well and pulled his tunic closer around him and his hood over his head. It wasn't cold enough for his cloak yet but he could tell it was getting close.

"There's where we can stay for the night." Jacob said, pointing.

"The ruins of D'Xel, are you insane Jacob?" exclaimed Aurella.

The ruined towers of D'Xel were clearly visible in the moonlight. It was the fortress of men built to fight against the ogres. At one time it was the easternmost outpost of men before they drove the ogres to the untamed jungles to the far east. Now the towers were long abandoned and loomed over them forbiddingly like three great monsters on the night horizon. The ogres laid siege to it for months, laying waste to it with catapults. In the dark you could still see where the walls stood.

"What's so bad about those old towers?" asked Thomas.

"They're haunted, everyone knows that." Aurella said.

Thomas rolled his eyes and shook his head. "I don't believe in ghosts and if we get inside for the night we'll have some protection from this cursed wind."

"Don't roll your eyes at me Thomas, I'm starting to like you."

"What he said, I don't believe in ghosts or ghouls and it's cold and windy." said Jacob and took off for the ruins.

"Ghosts?" questioned Brax. "I believe in ghosts, in fact I'm sure I saw some back at the lake." But Brax followed the other two regardless, the chill wind started to pick and the thought of comfort gave way to his fears.

Standing her ground, Aurella put her hands on her hips and she watched them as the trotted off boldly towards the towers, paying no heed to her at all. She was not about to be left alone though and she followed them to the towers, her pride ebbing.

Brax began to have his doubts again and he hesitated outside the doors, looking up at the blackened tower; black from age and soot from fires. Brax stood outside for a moment until a wolf howled and he quickly changed his mind again.

They made their camp on the first floor of the tower with the only door left standing. They shut the door and bolted it then climbed to the top floor. Spiral staircases led the way to the top and the night sky and stars were clearly visible through the nonexistent roof. Clearing hundred-year-old debris away to lay down their bedrolls, Aurella unrolled hers next to Thomas and got close to him.

"I'm scared." She explained.

"Certainly." Thomas said, not forgetting the kiss from her only yesterday. So much had happened since then.

Thomas fell asleep happily with Aurella in his arms and they all fell asleep quickly. But pervading Thomas's dreams was a silver dragon. Silver and shiny, his scales were beautiful like the sun. Thomas was no longer in the tower, but asleep in the middle of a rocky plane. 'Sleep Thomas, sleep…everything is all right', the dragon's kind words comforted him. Then the dragon rose up, snatching Thomas up in his talons, dangling him above his mouth ready to devour him in one bite. Thomas struggled helplessly in his dream but he awoke before his imminent death. Aurella stirred a little, her head still lay on his chest and he wiped the cold sweat from his forehead.

Unknown to them all, fifty feet below in the dark dreary dungeon of the D'Xel ruins a melfling rummaged around, looking for old forgotten treasure. He found a few coins here and there; enough for his next meal was all. If he could just find enough to buy a room with a fireplace at an inn and a bottle of wine, maybe even the comfort of a melfling woman. Moshki was ashamed of himself; he was a thief not an archeologist. If the Thieves Guild in Crossfalls saw him poking around the dirt for loose change they would disavow his membership.

"Oh now, here some real treasure!" Moshki said aloud, pushing open a pantry door not much taller than he was. He picked up a small round bottle and wiped off the dust from the mouth and popped the cork. Sniffing the contents like a fine connoisseur. "Rum!" he declared and took a small sip. "Seems a hundred years gave it a little kick."

Moshki knew the legends and ghost stories of the D'Xel ruins but he was a bit desperate at the moment. He was penniless and travelers to burgle were suspiciously absent along the road. What few people knew, underneath the ruins lay a vast system of tunnels, torture chambers and catacombs. Moshki fashioned a backpack out of some cloth and filled it with a few bottles of rum for later use and sat down to enjoy the rum. "Here's to you my friend." He said, nodding at the skeletal remains of a human lying near the pantry door. "Fine rum you kept here."

The next morning Jacob woke first, stretching loudly. His body stiff from sleeping on the hardwood floor, he stumbled to door opening it and looked out at the new day. The rising sun revealed something strange, the ground was moving, slithering. Dargons. He stood, shocked, there were at least seventy dargons crawling their way towards the towers. They must know we were here he thought and they must be coming for them.

"Get up!" he shouted to the others. "Get up! There are dargons outside hurry. They know were in here make haste."

The sudden thought of the dargons so near jolted them all into action.

"Barricade the door!" Thomas shouted as he grabbed a large stone and dropped it in front of the doorway to the tower.

"There must be fifty, maybe seventy of them outside, there's no way we can fight them all." Exclaimed Jacob.

Realization finally hit Brax and he began helping Thomas pile stones and anything else that they could find to barricade the door.

Aurella ran up the stairway to look out the windows on the second floor. The towers built for defense never had windows on the first floor. To her horror she saw the dargons stop crawling and go into a full gallop. Their mindlessness was driven by hunger and realizing their prey had caught onto the hunt they jumped up in unison and charged the tower doors.

"Hurry," Aurella cried out, "they're rushing full speed for us now!"

"More rocks." Ordered Thomas. "Help me with this big one."

Jacob grabbed the other end of the large carved brick and they both hurled it in front of the door.

The fastest dargon leaped into the air and threw itself at the door, using its head as a battering ram. The dargon rebounded off the door and fell to the stone steps leading to the entrance. A second one did the same as did a third but the fourth dargon hit the door with such force the door shook and splintered though thankfully only a little. After hitting the door, the large dargon fell shaking in convulsions. A piercing war cry rose from the dargons throats and more began ramming their heads at the barricaded door.

Aurella watched the horrific scene from her window. On the horizon she noticed a creature, unlike the other dargons; it stood upright like a human but it still had four legs. Its skin was red and leathery like some fabled demon. It had arms and hands and in one hand it held a staff. The creature paced back and forth as it watched the battle below.

The boys didn't stop piling rocks and debris in front of the door until they could no longer see it. Once finished, they ran back upstairs to look out the windows. Thomas stood next to Aurella and leaned out the window releasing an arrow into the dargon that was next in line for ramming duty. The dargon fell wounded on the stone steps. The dargons only became enraged and renewed their efforts to kill their prey held inside the tower. Jacob killed another and the dargon screams grew stronger.

"We don't have enough arrows." Brax said flatly, the impending doom sunk into his heart but he picked up his bow as well, making every shot count.

"We'll kill as many as we can from here, then charge them with our swords." Said Thomas.

"We have their anger now; the door is breaking." Jacob said.

Pulling her lute from off her back, Aurella began playing a tune. The song drifted down to the dargons below and she began chanting soft words. The dargons stopped their mindless attack and stopped throwing themselves against the door. Puzzled looks came across their faces and they stood dumbfounded looking up at Aurella as she played, a few of the dargons laid down and went to sleep.

Thomas stared at Aurella in amazement. "You're doing that to them? Making them go into a stupor?"

Aurella shook her head yes, not daring to stop the strumming of her finger nor her soft chants.

"Let's get out of here, then."

"They go back to their angered selves once the music stops." Even as she explained one of the dargons snarled and bared his fangs but it stopped once Aurella started playing again.

Odin watched the dargon attack on the tower ruins through Borgman's telescope. He looked on with mild amusement as the mere children were trying to fight off the dargons with only a few arrows but was surprised when he saw the girl begin playing her lute and the beasts were lulled into a drunken stupor, stumbling about on the ground and several just nodded off into sleep.

"Now is our time Borgman, we'll ride down and destroy the dargons. We'll appear as heroes in their sight and gain their trust. Once we find out where the key is we'll kill them."

Odin raised his fist in the air and motioned for the charge. "Into the fray!" he shouted.

"For sword and hammer!" the others shouted.

Even at his age old man Odin was fierce in battle. Raising his sword high and leading the charge the mesmerized dargons fell to him as he cleaved his way past several. The dargons died easily at first, not giving up a fight being under Aurella's charm but the spell was broken by the deafening sounds of battle and clanking armor. The Dargons turned on the cavalry but the dargon numbers were cut in half by the initial charge.

Odin looked back behind him, seeing that Dag had never left the safety of the hilltop. "Coward." He muttered.

What Odin didn't see was that Borgman rode up right beside him as he was slicing his way through the dargons. Borgman gave the old man a shove and Odin fell to the ground, stunned. He tried to stand but he had dropped his sword, he tried to grab it but as he did a dargon pounced on his arm tearing into his wrist another dargon jumped on his back, pinning him to the ground. Odin screamed in agony, trying desperately to stand. Yet another tore into his neck and Odin went limp. The feeding frenzy that followed was no sight for the weak. Aurella, Jacob, Brax and Thomas watched the whole scene from the second floor window in unbelief. The sight of a dargon walking off with the man's leg was forever seared into Aurella's mind. The other members of the Hammer came to his rescue but it was too late. They slew the dargons, knocking them off of Odin's limp body.

The armored men and horses drove a wedge through the remaining dargons and slew them all. The lead dargon, the one standing upright, tried to make escape up the hill, running directly past Dag who did nothing. One of the soldiers rode down the lead dargon on horseback driving a spear through it's back.

As the soldier returned he looked at Dag in disbelief wondering how the man had become a leader being the coward that he was.

The Brothers of the Hammer gathered around the pieces Odin Harbinger. The bodies of the dargons he killed lay about him in a pile. They were all dead now, their carcasses lay strewn about the courtyard.

Borgman dismounted removing the chain mail from his head. Looking down at the unmoving body of Odin Harbinger, Minister of Defense, leader of the Brotherhood of the Hammer and corrupt politician. "Is he dead?" he asked of the men gathered around Odin, he asked in earnest not of care.

"Yes sire."

"A pity, his position will be difficult to fill."

Borgman turned his attention towards the children still holed up in the tower. "You can come out now, all is safe."

Brax looked out the window of the second floor, they had all watched in amazement as the soldiers appeared out of nowhere to rescue them. They were no fools and were in no way going to leap out and greet these men. They had witnessed in horror as the man that was now trying to coax them out had killed the old man lying on the ground at that moment.

"It's safe I say." Shouted Borgman, smiling at the young boy whose head hung out the window. "All the dargons are dead, son."

"That banner, Thomas." said Brax. "That purple banner is the same one I saw in Greystone. These are the very men that laid our town to waste."

Thomas looked at the banner, purple satin with an embroidered dragon and underneath was a hammer crossed with a sword. Not forgetting for a second the purple scrap of satin he found snagged on the rail of his fence. Those were his mother's killers. Anger swelled inside him and he drew his bow.

Borgman continued to rant outside below. "Come out children, I bet you're hungry. We have some cheese and meat. We could get some tea going, we even have some wine." Borgman grew impatient. "I knew your father Thomas. My name is Chance Borgman."

"I knew your mother too." He said to quietly to himself.

He turned to the man beside him, "What was his stupid father's name?"

"Holden sir, Lord Holden Kray."

Borgman turned back to the window. "Holden and I fought together, side by side, in battle, Thomas."

Thomas let loose his arrow, aiming for Borgman's heart. Borgman saw the arrow coming and threw up his shield; the arrow penetrated the shield and nicked his arm. Borgman threw down his shield and grimaced at the blood that was drawn.

"Seems the boy knows you too, sire." Said the aide at his side.

"That little bastard. Kill them. Set the place on fire."

"Sir we can't kill them, we need the key and setting the place on fire would destroy the book. Not to mention The Prince wanted the boy alive." His aide reminded him.

"Dismantle the door, we'll take them alive." Borgman said, loud enough for the kids to hear.

"Is there a back way out of here?" Aurella asked.

"I didn't see anything." Said Jacob. "We will need to barricade the door more; we'll never be able to fight them."

"I'll help." Said Brax and they both bounded down the spiral staircase.

Brax ran at break neck speed down to the first floor and when he reached the fourth step from the bottom he jumped to the floor. This was a habit he performed a hundred times at his own home at the inn and brewery his father owned, jumping that fourth step to the floor. The floorboards in the old ruined tower were not strong and when Brax landed the floor caved and collapsed under the weight slowly at first and Brax attempted to hold his balance and leap forward, but Jacob who was right behind him couldn't stop in time colliding into Brax and they both plummeted through the rotted floorboards.Both boys fell the ten feet into the hidden dungeon tunnels below. Both fell hard and stunned and began rolling down the earthen stairs that seemed to keep going and going. Brax and Jacob hit every step for fifty feet.

Thomas and Aurella, hearing the crashing noises immediately thought that Jacob and Brax were in trouble and ran to their defense and met the same falling fate as their predecessors.Unknowing and not very grateful either, these events saved them. They weren't appreciative of this small hand of fate that saved them from being dragged to Mission Keep and most certainly imprisoned and they certainly didn't know their adventures were only beginning.

Chapter 6

A dungeon is no place for children to play.

The hand of the Lord was upon me, and carried me out in the spirit of the Lord, and set me down in the midst of the valley, which was full of bones, and caused me to pass by them roundabout: and lo, they were very dry. And he said to me, Son of man, can these bones live? and I answered, O Lord God, thou knowest.

-Ezekiel 37:1-3.

Moshki, still slightly hung over from hundred-year-old rum, was unaware of the dargon attacks and the humans above him and would have stayed blissfully ignorant of both until four humans tumbled down upon him. Luckily only Aurella landed on him, being the lightest of the four, if any of those other hairless apes would have landed on him, he certainly would have been crushed. Still neither of them found the moment pleasurable. Aurella had dealt with melflings before, talked with them, sang and even laughed with them but the unexpected landing on this hapless melfling and the preceding moment's events were all that she could handle. So in order to hold on to her sanity she let out a scream. Moshki equally rattled, screamed as well, turned and ran into the darkness of the tunnel.

All watched the melfling run away in awe and only Thomas maintained his wits. "We need to run, that door won't hold forever, those men are after us."

"Where?" asked Brax.

"Follow the melfling." Thomas shrugged.

They all started running thru the maze of the dungeon, following the melfling who in turn thought the four clumsy humans were chasing him. Which, they were after him in a sense, but not to hurt him. Moshki couldn't understand why because he knew he had never stolen anything from them, he made it a point never to thieve from children, mostly because they never had anything of value than out of ethics. You try pick pocketing a kid; you wound up the successful owner of a handful of sticky candy and lint. Moshki ran on thru the tunnel in the darkness as fast as his little legs could possibly carry him, he was slow but he had the advantage of having keen night vision.

Borgman paced rapidly back and forth in the courtyard in front of the tower, at one time it had been a beautiful garden but thorns and death choked any beauty that once fell upon this place. The men worked at the door, prying loose the old rusted hinges from the stone, and the old oaken slab fell on the steps below. This only revealed the pile of debris the boys labored on earlier and the Soldiers of the Hammer began clearing the way.

"Sir." Dag Sinjan interrupted Borgman's pacing. "Some of the men want to know if they can bury Odin's body."

"What?" snapped Borgman. Who seemed to be in a mesmeric state of his own.

"Bury him, sir." Dag leaned over and whispered into Borgman's ear. "Ruddy good work, sir, I saw you from the hill."

"Of course you did, Dag. You never left the hill."

"I'm a naval man, you know that, swords and horseback riding are for you army fellows."

Borgman stared blankly at Dag again.

"The body, can we bury Odin, he's been laying out in that mangled state for hours in the sun and frankly it's beginning to make the men uneasy."

"Right, right. Sorry for the jab. Have the men bury him but do it in haste. Those kids will be our prisoners soon as were thru the door."

"Yes sir. You will most likely replace Odin as leader of the Hammer. It would be a considerable promotion, not to mention the prestige that goes with it. No Minister of the Fifth Column has ever been appointed leader of the Brotherhood of the Hammer before."

"Yes indeed." Replied Borgman.

"If you would need a right hand man, I would like to offer up my services. Lest say, the events of this morning be revealed. If the news of the murder of Odin were to leak out, it would be unfortunate."

Borgman grimaced; the little worm was blackmailing him. "For certain, I need a man of your … qualities. When we return to Storm Gap, you will receive due recompense."

"Thank you, sir." Dag said smiling.

"Were through the door sire." Said one of the soldiers running up to him.

"Well don't waste time telling me, fool. Get the boy, retrieve the book." Borgman said, while motioning with his hand.

The soldier hesitated, knowing the display of ire that was to follow. "We can't sire. It appears they are no longer in the tower."

A sour look grew across Borgman's face, his brow furrowed and his fists clenched.

"Did they vanish? Sprout wings and fly away?"

"No sir, seems they escaped through a large hole in the floor that appears to lead to an underground system. We would follow and give pursuit but the first step is a rather big one."

"Providence has been on this boy's side from the beginning. How does he manage to elude us?"

"I don't know sir."

"The question was rhetorical and certainly I would never ask a fool such as you for advice or answers." Said Borgman. "Get some rope, we'll get down this hole and with any luck they're lying dead on the bottom."

"Stop!" cried out Aurella.

"What is it?" asked Thomas.

"I can't see anymore." She said.

"I can't see either." Said Thomas.

The small group had run but a short distance before running out of visibility. They followed the melfling for some time but he disappeared into the darkness and now no one knew which way to turn. The corridor ran straight for a while but then forked, Thomas was sure they made two rights and they passed a few dozen doors neatly spaced closely together. Then a left, then straight but then it really didn't matter because they couldn't turn back.

"That poor melfling." Said Aurella. "I think I scared him more than he scared me."

"I'm sure he's ok." Said Thomas.

"Melfling!" Aurella's voice echoed down the corridor. "I'm really sorry for landing on you."

"I don't think that's terribly wise, Aurella." Said Jacob.

"Yes, I agree with Jacob." Said Thomas. "Those men are after me for some reason and I don't know why. But shouting down the hall for that melfling could lead those men to us, they'll get through that door eventually."

Aurella ignored the both of them. "Melfling!" Aurella shouted again. "We're terribly, terribly sorry for frightening you but we meant you no harm and if you could show us the way out of here we can reward you."

"The name is Moshki, that is me." Moshki stepped forth from the shadows of the dark, while he was perfectly able to see in the dark, he knew that they couldn't and accommodated them. He stopped running as soon as they did. His chubby little body was in no shape for long distance running. It was only by shear will and fear that he made it as far as he did and now he stood not ten feet before them panting and trying to catch his breath. He listened to their conversations and discerned that they weren't trying to kill, eat or otherwise rob him and indeed they were only irritating.

The company was a bit startled when Moshki calmly spoke up so close to them. He leaned on one arm stretched out against the wall, still regaining his breath and composure. "I'll help, no problem." He said. "I don't need payment for the services, I know you don't have any. Just stop chasing me."

"Thank you." Aurella gushed, rushing over to Moshki to give him a big hug, which he accepted with big pleasure and a smile on his face. Moshki loved the women and liked to put on the charms; even if they were human or melfling.

"I hope this helps you see a little bit better." Moshki pulled a match from his pocket and lit one of the nearby torches that lined the underground tunnel system.

"We weren't really chasing you." explained Thomas. "You see there are men back there and they're chasing us, well me really. I think they mean to kill me for what or why I don't know. In fact, I'm sure that they killed my mother…"

Thomas stopped short when he realized he was carrying on a conversation with a two-foot tall, long eared fuzzy mouse. Thomas had never even heard of melflings, though it was obvious Aurella did. Under the circumstances it all seemed rather bizarre.

Moshki put his small paw up motioning to Thomas, "It's ok, you don't have to go into details. I've been chased a few times myself. Mostly out of towns, never through a dungeon but it's all well."

Inside Moshki breathed a sigh of relief that his newfound friends were fellow rogues and on the run from the law like himself and not some vigilante group still chasing him from the previous town.

They followed Moshki through the deep tunnels of the dungeon, upstairs and down, through iron doors and passed prison cells. The halls were filled with cobwebs and lined with broken bones. Aurella shuddered at the thought, that humans were kept down here but when she looked inside one of the cells, she saw the hanging bones were not human at all, but the bones of ogres. The cruelty that occurred was no less comforting that the victims of this dungeon were ogres. The eight-foot tall skeletons hung from their arms, bound at their wrists with iron clasps.

Moshki told them all about his life in Crossfalls, he explained how, as mayor of the small village, he built it into a thriving jewel on the frontier, a trading post where all travelers passed through on their way to the east and to the west. He told them how a jealous rival kicked him out of the town. It wasn't the truth by any stretch of the imagination, but Moshki enjoyed tall tales, especially ones involving him.

"Did you hear that?" asked Thomas, he stopped walking and put his ear to the stone tunnel wall.

"Hear what, Thomas?" Aurella asked.

But they all stopped moving and could hear the clanking of armor and footsteps behind them.

"What do we do? They're still following us." She said.

"Run to that archway!" Thomas yelled.

Grabbing the femur of an ogre long past, Thomas began hitting the top center stone of the archway with all his might. Braxton and Jacob did the same and Aurella began kicking the sides of the archway, even Moshki offered his advice, pointing at different weak points in the archway. The center stone came crashing down, as did the rocks above, then more masonry came down all around and they realized they began a reaction that would quickly become out of control. A look of horror crept over their faces and no one needed to say run at that moment, they all turned and ran down the tunnel with all their might. Moshki was not happy about having to give forth the physical effort once more. It occurred to him that he had to run quite a bit these days and he really didn't like it.

Dust and debris rolled down behind them as they ran, but they only had to run a short distance, the avalanche stopped nearly as soon as it began. They looked behind them to see that the hall was completely blocked and they all began to cheer.

"There's no way they can follow us after that!" Thomas said triumphantly.

"Of course, we might also be blocked in." Moshki said flatly, twitching his nose.

All eyes turned on Moshki and Jacob was the first to speak.

"I thought you were leading us to the back way out?" he asked.

"I've never been here before," Moshki explained. "I don't know if there is a back way or not."

"For the love of the Goddess Thena, why didn't you tell us before?" asked Aurella.

"Don't fret dear." Moshki backtracked. "These old dungeons always have a rear entrance; these tunnels were made just as much for torture as they were for a hasty retreat. Unfortunately, sometimes the doors out can be secret, hidden, or even locked so tight no one can get in or out without the key."

"So what do we do?" asked Aurella, becoming flustered.

"We try and find it, if it's locked hopefully I am able to get around it and we slip out into the great wide open plains of Arnok with freedom before us."

"And if we can't find it?" asked Thomas.

"Well, then we're doomed to wonder these halls and die a horrible death of starvation and join the bones littering these halls."

"Let's find the back door." Thomas offered.

"A fine idea sir." Moshki said.

"If we start to get hungry, let's eat the Melfling." Brax muttered quietly, thinking he couldn't hear, but Moshki was used to such remarks and let it pass.

Borgman surveyed the new obstacle brought down before him, the dungeon hallway was completely blocked and it was certain that it would take two weeks' worth of excavating to clear it. Those kids were only feet away from him this time and the damned boy escaped his grasp at every turn.

Ulysses approached Borgman, he was the only one who wasn't afraid of him at the time. "I really think we should turn back, milord."

"Can't you clear the way with your magic, you are a mage aren't you?" Borgman's anger grew with each passing second.

"My art is in the realm of summoning, such things like fire balls, monsters… small demons."

"Summon a golem to clear the path!" Borgman ordered.

"Summoning golems can be a hazardous feat sir, they are very temperamental and can easily turn on anyone nearby and they don't follow orders well at all. When I've summoned them in the past, I make sure I'm at least a hundred feet away from the point it enters our world."

"Is there anything you can do at all?" growled Borgman.

"I've summoned hordes of gnomes before sir, but even a horde of gnomes would be hard pressed to get through all this rubble in a week's time."

"Think of something, damn you."

"Sir, I'm starting to get an uneasy feeling about these tunnels. I think we should return immediately, get our horses and look for the back entrance to this foul dungeon on the outside. It will be dark very soon, and after a certain hour…" he paused.

"Well, what after a certain hour?"

"Nasties come out, evil ghosts, the dead rise…that sort of thing. Ogres were tortured in these dungeons years ago, I don't want to face them."

Borgman turned on his heels, and headed back the way they came without saying another word. The rest of his delegation followed him, murmuring to each other.

The company of adventurers reached a large alcove, they knew it was getting late in the day even though there were deep below when the sunset. Moshki instinctively knew that this had to be the way out; he had been in many a dungeon before. The door to the alcove was locked, but as he promised he knew his way around these things.

"Let me have a go at it." Moshki said, relieved that he never left home without his lock picks, he pulled a short hooked one and deftly opened the portal. There was a door that clearly led outside on the far end, preceded by a long row of steps that led up and out. The moonlight was clearly visible through the barred window and they could feel the soft cool air blowing through. There at the top of the steps, before the door laid the bones of some long forgotten guard.

They all breathed a sigh of relief and began climbing, but as they did an apparition rose from the pile of bones that lay before the door, like smoke from a heavy laden pipe. The travelers stood in frozen terror before the ghost as he took shape before their eyes. Like a thin wisp, it took on the shape of an old haggard guard dressed in the rags that he died in so many years ago. The room grew colder and he cast his tired gaze down upon them, speaking.

"What news of the battle?" the ghost cried out to them.

They stood before him, speechless and motionless. Moshki began slowly inching his way backwards towards the door they had come through. When the ghost didn't get an answer he asked once more with much sorrow in his voice. "The tide of the battle, are we winning or have the ogres gained the ground?"

"The battle is over master guard." Said Thomas. "The day was won by men, we pushed the ogres to the far east and have not heard much of them since.

"I am much relieved to hear the message, good boy. It seems I have waited a long time to hear the news." Said the ghastly guard. "And what of Anthion, is he ok?"

"I don't know, I'm sorry."

"Anthion is a dear friend and fellow guard, he volunteered to join in the fight. I'm still waiting to be relieved of my guard. Have you heard whether they have sent a replacement? I'm really very tired."

"We don't know of your replacement, again I am sorry." Said Thomas.

"If you would be so kind as let us pass, sir ghost, we will trouble you no more and be on our way." Said Aurella.

"Ghost, Ghost! To whom are you referring to as a ghost?" The apparition looked around in puzzlement but then looked down at the bones that lay at his feet. A deep sadness came over him as he realized that he was gazing down at his own bones lying on the floor, a rusted scimitar clutched in a bony hand, and his uniform, now rotted and moldy.

"A guard's duty is to never leave his post until properly relieved." The ghost began to weep. "I grew so hungry…so weary."

"We are very sorry, if you let us pass, we promise we will try and find Anthion."

"You may pass, children. Be well." The ghost opened the door for them then faded back to the bones from where he rose and finally Thomas's heart stopped pounding so hard.

"You're very handy for a town mayor." Braxton said cynically, breaking the feeling of dread they had all just encountered. "Picked that lock like a professional."

"I'm just glad you don't have to eat me for dinner, Brax."

Aurella smiled at Moshki, and she knew that would be friends.

The crew left the dank dungeon and they were happy to be out in the night air, even though it was little cool. The dungeon exit came out miles away from the towers, and they knew they would be safe to rest there for the night. Their pursuers would have to backtrack miles; they had put a good day and half distance travel between them.

Borgman returned down the corridor from where they came. They all knew it would be hours until they got out and it was very late but none of them considered bedding down in this place for evening. But the witching hour came upon them and they were still in depths of the dungeon.

One of Borgman's men glanced over into one of the cells and noticed that ogre bones had come alive and once more began to struggle to get out of their captivity. The man couldn't help it and let out scream not unlike a woman's. A skeletal hand thrust through the bars in the window, grabbing Dag Sinjan by his throat. Borgman and the other men looked on in horror but did nothing to rescue him, it was each to his own in their survival and they all began running. Dag tried to scream but the skeletal grip was too tight. His face grew purple. More skeletal hands reached through the bars, pulling him and ripping his body to shreds, what was left of him was pulled through the bars and the ogre skeletons roared in victory.

Borgman and his men began running, shedding their armor as they went to lose weight and gain the ability to run faster. Another ogre skeleton rose up before them, this one was not behind bars, it grabbed the man that was out front by his neck with such force that the rest of his body was separated from his head and the body fell nervously kicking on the dirty floor. Ulysses extended his hands out, summoning a small ball of flame and sent it flying at the skeleton ogre, it exploded into several thousand pieces and the men kept running. They were now in a panic for their own lives, their survival. The ogres were reaping their vengeance on Borgman and his men.

They kept running through the night, and escaped back out the way they came in the early morning hours, there was only Ulysses and Borgman left as they collapsed out into the light. They slept in complete exhaustion. Borgman did not where or how he had lost the other men, he thought they were somewhere behind him but they never emerged. He had to return to Storm Gap empty handed, and no men left. A third of the Brotherhood of the Hammer was now gone and he would have to return and find suitable replacements.

Ulysses stood up panting. "That was crazy." Was all he could muster to say.

Chapter 7

A fine war

And we are here as on a darkling plain Swept with confusedm alarms of struggle and fight Where ignorant armies clash by night.

- Matthew Arnold

A fairy no taller than Thomas's hand flittered curiously around the company of strangers asleep on a grassy hill. She tilted her head to one side examining each teenager and one overgrown mouse carefully, wondering what brought them to such a desolate plain. Kris was her name and she loved all manner of things shiny. She settled on the fat mouse and watched him as he twitched his whiskers in restless sleep. He'll do, she decided and delved into his vest pocket in search of shiny things. Struggling, Kris came out a few seconds later towing a small gold coin with her. She could barely stay in flight as she dropped the coin to the ground. She was all disheveled after the pocket diving experience; she combed her straight black hair back and pulled up her black and white stockings on her left leg, checking herself in the reflection of the gold coin. Placing the coin on edge, she rolled it down the hill to her small home at the bottom, her presence undetected by the company of strangers.

Thomas woke first, his head hurt and his neck was stiff and bad dreams invaded his slumber in the previous evenings sleep. The ghosts of old soldiers stood before him, crying to him and all he could say were the feeble words that he was sorry. Then the dragon appeared once more and only laughed at the soldiers. Then he awoke.

He wiped the crust from his eyes and looked over at Aurella, who was not at all disturbed by the cold morning air. He scavenged around the area and luckily found a few eggs from a bird of unknown origin. He chanced a small fire to warm them and the others began to stir. Moshki woke next, his

nose began to twitch at the smell of eggs cooking.

"We are in deep gratitude for your help, melfling." Said Thomas. "We would never have made it out alive without you."

"Please, please. Call me Moshki." He replied. "You did fairly well yourself back there, you stopped those soldiers from capturing us and you talked your way passed that ghost. You know when to fight and when to negotiate, those are good qualities."

"Thank you, Moshki."

"And what shall I call you, sir knight."

"I am Thomas Kray, just call me Thomas. The slumbering angel is Aurella, that's her brother Jacob who's waking now and the oaf is my best friend Brax."

"You like the girl; I could tell right off the way you look at each other."

"Yes, I think I love her."

"You think? Why do you just think you love her, you don't know?"

"Well, you see I've never been in love before. I don't know what is I'm feeling."

"I see." Said Moshki. "Let me give you some advice and some help from one who is has been in love a hundred times. I fall in love every time a pretty melfling girl passes by me. In fact, I fell in love with one just the other day, confound it, I wish I could remember her name. Chrissie, Kristy, Crystal… something like that."

"What does love feel like?" asked Thomas, trying to get him back on track.

"Really it feels awful, just awful. You get sweaty, your heart beats too fast, your stomach hurts and your brain never engages to full capacity and can't say what you want to say."

"And you do this all the time, you say?"

"Yes, indeed. It's a terrible disease."

"Well, I'm in love then, I have all those horrible symptoms. But then why fall in love?"

Moshki put his hand to his chin in deep thoughtfulness. "Katrina! That was her name."

Thomas only smiled and then the rest woke up. "Keep this between us, Moshki." Thomas said, putting his finger to his lips. A knowing smile crept over Moshki's face and he gave Thomas a thumbs up and a wink.

"I will, I keep a tight mouth, I do. Never say a word, that's my motto."

They all ate ravenously and the hot meal gave their spirits a boost but they did not linger, the fire was a huge chance, even though it was small it could attract dargons, thieves and the men that were chasing them. They all felt good about having some distance between them and Borgman's men, except for Thomas who felt he missed his chance at revenge. Thomas would have taken a little solace knowing that almost all of Borgman's men were dead, ripped apart by the skeletons of ogres, because he wanted to do the deed. They broke camp and headed down the hill where the dungeon tunnel ended.

"Moshki," Aurella said. "We are all traveling by ship to Trilliane; we welcome your company if you would travel with us, at least to the Port of Korinth."

"Aye," Said Thomas. "We could use an ex-mayor who can pick locks."

"I would be honored; the land is too hazardous nowadays. Even Trilliane sounds appealing."

"There should be an old road that cuts through the Arnok Plain." Jacob said. "We should just have to go north a little while, and then we can cut back south to Crossfalls."

"Crossfalls?" Moshki gasped.

"Don't worry little one." Aurella said laughing. "We shall give you clever disguise, so that ex-mayors need not be run out of town again."

"Clever disguise?" Laughed Moshki. "All I need to do is change my vest, you fools of humans cannot tell one melfling from the next."

They only had to go north a short distance before finding the old road that led back to Crossfalls. A hundred years ago there was plenty of trade between Crossfalls, the Citadel and the Towers D'Xel but the road stopped getting used some time back, the Citadel did all its trade with Mission Keep and soon the road became overgrown.

Squinting his eyes, Brax looked out on the horizon. "What's that thar in the distance?" He said pointing.

The all looked on, but they all could see was a cloud of dust rising up in the distance. There were men on horseback, leading the way, carrying battle streamers and banners. These men were different from Borgman's men, their armor was black and their banners were yellow and red. Behind the banner bearers was an imposing man who rode alone; his armor was black as coal as were his eyes. His face was like stone and behind him his army followed. He was General Du'Beck, leader of the East Army. His men marched faithfully and triumphantly behind him on foot and on horseback in four columns wide down the old road, they numbered ten thousand strong.

The General, although weathered and hard, was not arrogant and took immediate notice of the strange group of travelers on a road since forgotten. He held up his right hand and the army stopped their march, the sounds of trumpets signaled the halt. He raised a suspicious eye on three young men, a girl and of all things a melfling. They were going in the wrong direction for a fight.

"Sergeant Major!" he called out.

An equally grizzled and hard man trotted forward on his horse. He carried a lance that bore many battle streamers. He too looked at the strange travelers standing alongside the road.

Thomas, Aurella, Brax, Jacob and Moshki stood in awe at the sight of such a vast army; it was the most men and women any of them had ever seen. Indeed, there were both men and women clad in armor and bearing swords and spear as well. They were also shocked that such a large army, obviously on its way north to do battle with the dargons, would stop and pay homage to four kids and a melfling.

"Greetings travelers. I am General Du'Beck, leader of the East Army. Congratulations."

The General turned his horse, and cried out "Forward, ho."

They all looked a little puzzled and Moshki was the first to speak up. "Congratulations, why did he say congratulations to us?" Moshki said, referring his question to the Sergeant Major.

The Sergeant Major didn't answer; he just eyed them up and down for a brief moment as the army marched passed them row upon row. The battle streamers made an uneasy whipping sound from the strong breeze blowing across the plain. At last he spoke.

"Welcome to the East Army, the greatest, the strongest and the most powerful army ever to march. You will solemnly swear to fight, to uphold our truths, to defend our banner, and you will obey all orders by your superiors. You will march twenty miles a day, and you will like it. You will carry a full laden pack, your weapon, and anything else we deem necessary. There will be no complaining. You are now soldiers of the East Army. Again, congratulations."

Moshki blinked. The severity of the moment was lost on him and as usual and he couldn't help saying something. "But I'm a melfling, we don't fight."

"You'll shut your pie hole!"

Better sense grabbed hold of Moshki and he shut his pie hole.

The Sergeant Major turned his horse and yelled at the first noncommissioned officer he saw. "Corporal!"

A nervous young soldier with two stripes painted on his armored sleeves ran forward and reported to the Sergeant Major. "Corporal Winguard reporting as ordered Sergeant Major!"

Corporal Winguard was a dark skinned young man with a face that showed little emotion.

"Show these two," he paused pointing to Jacob and Thomas. "to the Ranger Battalion. The girl… to the Templars."

He paused and pointed to Braxton. "That one, to First Brigade. Enlist who you must to carry this out."

"And what of the melfling, Sergeant Major?"

The Sergeant Major paused even longer, scratching his clean-shaven chin. "He shall be a litter bearer for the Templars." The Sergeant Major prided himself on his knack for being able to place a soldier into the right position, and he knew he had done a good job in with this motley looking group.

Corporal Winguard wasted no time in carrying out his orders; he enlisted a Private to show Braxton to First Brigade. They had to run, because the army did not pause their marching just because it had five new recruits and First Brigade was in the front. Brax was actually excited about the sudden change of plans, soldiering always seemed like it would be a thrill and he couldn't wait to receive his armor.

Corporal Winguard showed Thomas and Jacob to the Ranger Battalion while Aurella and Moshki followed in stunned silence. She had no desires to be a soldier, to fight or to see blood spilt on the ground.

"Nope." said Moshki who shared Aurella's feelings. "Not going to do this, nope."

"Shh, Moshki." Cautioned Thomas.

Moshki didn't stop and kept ranting. "I am leaving the minute the sun sets. I'm out of here; I'm not going to fight. I'm not going to be somebody's litter bearer. It's just not in my blood."

"If I might offer a word of advice. Don't leave." Said Corporal Winguard.

"See, he heard you." Cautioned Thomas.

"It's alright, I won't tell. I was in your boots a year ago. I was just walking along, whistling a song and they snatched me up." He said shaking his head. "But if you run... and some have tried, they hunt you down. They're relentless. The army has special team of hunters, just to get deserters. They drag you back, kicking and screaming, and then… they hang you."

Moshki gulped.

"They hang you up by a rope around your neck, right in front of the entire army. A sign is nailed to your chest with in big red letters, deserter. Then everyone marches past to take a gander at your dead corpse."

"Do you have many deserters?" Asked Jacob.

"Only new recruits too stupid to heed my advice."

The words did little to comfort Aurella, and at last Moshki was speechless.

"Someone should tell Brax about that." Aurella said.

"I don't think we have to worry about Brax," said Thomas. "He looked more excited than a child in a toy Shoppe."

Jacob and Thomas were dropped at the Ranger Battalion with little fan fair. An older looking lieutenant took charge of them as Corporal Winguard turned them over, saluting the officer crisply. The officer eyed Jacob and Thomas with apparent disdain.

"More kids." He said under his breath as he was walking. "Come with me."

The boys followed the Ranger lieutenant at a near run to a large caravan wagon being pulled by a full team of horses. The lieutenant jumped aboard and motioned them to follow. The wagon was large, and served as a mobile office. The lieutenant sat down, and began rummaging around a small makeshift desk.

Unlike the other soldiers, the Rangers did not wear armor and the lieutenant sitting before them was no different. He sat behind a table as he handed the boys papers to sign. He was impressive and scary looking Thomas thought. A scar ran down his face starting from over his right eye and crawled down to his cheek. His leather tunic was speckled green, grey and brown, which enabled him to blend into any type of terrain and underneath, was silver chain mail.

"I see you don't need any weapons; I pray that you can use them. A ranger is a different breed of warrior; our job is to scout and to disengage the enemy whenever possible. It is imperative that you report the information back to headquarters immediately."

"Yes sir." They chimed together rather awkwardly.

"Sign these." He ordered, handing them the papers.

The good corporal brought Aurella and Moshki to the Templar Knights, an order of men and women who were dedicated to healing but they also fought, they were known for their bravery in battle by rushing to the aid of a fallen soldier, fighting their way if needed. Standing before Aurella was the commander of the Knights, possibly the most beautiful woman Aurella had ever seen. She was tall, taller than most men with cascading blonde hair coming down across her blue armor. A white cloak was draped across her back, emblazoned with a red cross, the symbol of the Knights Templar. She looked down upon Aurella and smiled, but then cast a curious look at Moshki.

"What am I supposed to do with a melfling, corporal?"

"Blame the Sergeant Major, ma'am. I deliver them, I don't choose them." He saluted the commander and bid Aurella and Moshki good luck.

"I believe the Sergeant Major intended me to be a litter bearer, m' lady. Whatever position that entails, I am sure I am unsuited for it, and will gladly bid you farewell and trouble you no more." Moshki said with flourish.

"You are most certainly unfit for carrying bodies back from battle; however, you may not leave under any circumstance. There is war at hand and every good soul is needed. The Sergeant Major has an intense dislike for me, and loves to play his little games, however you are here and I will most certainly find a job for you melfling." She turned her attention to Aurella. "I am Captain Serena, commander of the Knights Templar. You will begin your instruction in the art of healing after you draw some gear."

"My name is Aurella," She said bowing. "I am well versed in healing, lady. I make potions from adder's tongue and golden seal for healing and I know how to bind wounds. My father taught me everything and I have also studied many books. Even more, I've been told my songs have the power of healing."

"We will see how well you perform, child." She said curtly. "Now off to the quarter master with ye, draw your armor and a sword."

Aurella started running. Moshki followed her like a lost puppy, he had no plans of letting Aurella out of his sight, and he felt obligated to her now. Aurella abruptly stopped and turned around to Serena, "But where is this quartermaster?" she called out to her, sheepishly realizing that she was running and no idea of where she was going.

Serena didn't speak, and just pointed at a large colorful caravan, one even larger than the one that Thomas was currently in, and twice the team of horses pulling it.

It was hours since they were forced into compulsory service, they marched on foot through the day and into the early evening till they finally made camp. Aurella and Moshki were wondering about their friends, and wishing for a horse.

"My paws are killing me." Exclaimed Moshki.

"As are mine," said Aurella, "my feet I mean, I don't think I would want paws. No offense of course."

"Paws are a wonderful thing, when they aren't forced to march. For instance, my paws are as useful as my hands, I can open a bottle of port or stuff a pipe with them. Can you do that, human girl?

"No, of course not."

"See, there you go."

"I beg your pardon; feet are not totally useless. I can, kick with them and…" Aurella paused a moment, unable to think of something else her feet could do besides the obvious running and walking.

"And?"

"I'm thinking, Moshki." She paused a second more and gave up. "Oh bother, I wouldn't need to open a bottle of port or stuff a pipe anyways." She laughed.

Moshki laughed with her. "How do you think our friends our doing?"

"They are probably fairing just the same, sore feet and backs."

"I'm hungry too." Complained Moshki.

"Pushups Mr. Thomas, Mr. Jacob," ordered the ranger lieutenant. "Lots and lots of pushups."

"Yes sir." They said in unison.

The ranger Lieutenant was a hardened man, and the boys didn't know his name. He never offered up who he was. They heard that no one knew his name, and that's the way he liked it.

"You don't like being here, do you?

"No sir." Thomas shouted, alone.

"I think that was rhetorical." Jacob whispered.

"You don't like being here?" The Lieutenant yelled. "I need to make you into soldiers. I don't care if you don't like being here, you are here to stay. When I am through with you, you will be soldiers. Stop your pushups."

"Thank you, sir."

"I need you to go out on a scouting patrol. I want you to head just north of the setting sun."

The boys were exhausted from the all-day march, but they did not protest. They had learned to keep their mouths closed whenever it came to opinions or protests.

"Grab some chow from the cook and take it with you, we have no time for sitting around relaxing to enjoy your dinner."

"I wish I had a mirror to see how I look." Brax said to a fellow grunt soldier, while he was trying to admire himself and looking down at his armor. The armor he was wearing was blackened to stop the glare of the sun. He had received an issue sword but he kept his old one. The issued one was worn and did not have an edge and the steel it was made from was of poor quality. His new shield however was something of beauty; it was blackened like his armor, and it had the faint image of a winged angel.

"This shield could stop a hundred dargons." Brax said to his new found friend.

"Let me help you," said the other soldier, "you definitely look like a newb soldier, your armor has no chinks, and your face has no scars. If you had a mirror you would only stare and kiss yourself."

Brax ignored him, "I'm going to show the others what a warrior looks like."

Brax strode out in the encampment as if it belonged to him and he was the general of the East Army. He passed several young female soldiers who giggled. Brax considered their giggling as a sign of admiration but they were laughing at his foolish bravado. He walked to the ranger camp, only to discover that Thomas and Jacob were out on patrol, no doubt looking for any sign of dargons. Maybe they would see some action soon he hoped. He continued on to the Templars in hopes of bumping into Moshki and Aurella.

Aurella was sitting alone, she was busy making healing salves and would not have even noticed Brax walking up to her if it were not for his loud demeanor.

"Look at you," she said, "you're all shiny and proud. And what do I owe the pleasure of your company?"

"I wanted to apologized to you. I'm sorry we got off on the wrong start."

Aurella smiled. "It's ok, I understand."

"I guess I was pretty jealous of you two. Thomas is my best friend; I don't want to lose him."

"You know; we can be friends as well."

"That would be great."

Moshki was sitting off to the side taking in the conversation. Humans are complicated bunch, he wondered if he would ever be able to understand them.

Jacob motioned for Thomas to look at the ground. "How many do you think there are?" He asked.

"Must be thirty or forty at least."

"Aye, that's my estimation as well, along with the herd trails we've found there must be a hundreds in this area."

"This is more than just scouting parties. There's an army of them coming."

"We better get back and report this, it's getting late as it is."

They entered into the camp feeling pretty tired but satisfied they did a good job. They rushed as fast as their sore feet could take them to get to the ranger commander. They rushed into his tent to give the captain the news.

The captain however was not pleased. "How dare you rush into my tent like this!" He bellowed.

Thomas worked up the nerve to speak. "Sir, sorry for the intrusion but we have urgent news."

He paused staring at them. "Well spit it out, there's not much sunlight left in this day."

"Sir, there's a large dargon force coming. Hundreds maybe more." Thomas said.

"That's just what we saw in the north part of here, just a few kilometers away. There may be even more, maybe thousands." Jacob said.

The captain didn't say a word, he stroked his clean shaven chin and glared at them. "I see. So you expect me to believe to newbs on their first day of the job claim there are hundreds. Maybe even thousands of dargons surrounding us.

Thomas looked, rather stony faced. "Well in a word. Yes."

"Get the hell out of my tent."

"Sir?"

"Get out before I lose self-control and throw you out in the mud."

Thomas and Jacob walked back to their sleeping tent, they were tired. "This could be bad." Thomas said.

"Yeah, he sure didn't want to hear what we had to say."

They grabbed some food and head back to their tents eating while they walked. The food was some kind of non-descript mush with a big hunk of back bacon. The food was hardly edible but they gulped it down like it was their last meal. Jacob stopped eating at stared at his bowl.

"What's the matter?" Thomas asked.

"There's a fly in my slop."

"Lucky you, extra protein."

Jacob looked once more at the bowl, winced with a wrinkled up nose. He carefully scooped out the fly and resumed eating.

"I maybe hungry but a fly is still a little bit too …."

"Disgusting?"

"Yep, that's the word."

On their way they ran into Brax who was looking pretty tired himself.

"What's up Brax?"

"Just got done with D and C." He said exuberantly.

"What's D and C?" Jacob asked.

"Drill and ceremony." He responded rather proudly.

"What's drill and ceremony?" Thomas asked.

Brax huffed at the question. "Drill and ceremony is where you march around in formation and in step while presenting your sword."

"I see. Sounds rather boring. So that's what you were doing while we were out on an actual mission." Thomas said flatly.

Brax took a moment and thought about it. "Now that you mention it, it was pretty bad. We just marched around in circles while some sergeant yelled at us for being out of step."

"To be honest, scouting around in the hot sun wasn't that exciting either." Thomas confessed. "We're worried, we found a lot of dargon tracks. There must be hundreds out there right now."

"Aye, and when we told the captain about it he kicked us out of his tent and called us newbs." Jacob interjected.

"You are a couple of newbs." Brax laughed. "Thomas, I want to tell you something."

Thomas was concerned about the odd request. Brax never asked to say something, he just blurted it out. "Go ahead. What is it?"

"I went to see Aurella this morning."

Now Thomas was really taken aback. "You went to see Aurella. Why?"

"I wanted to apologize to her. I've been acting like an ass, and I want to apologize to you too. You like her and that's fine."

Thomas laughed. "So I have your blessing now? Thanks dad."

"Well you don't have mine yet." Jacob stated protectively.

"Not yet, I will." Thomas said confidently smiling.

"Anyway, she's in the Templar's tent with Moshki."

"Maybe I'll see her later." Thomas said.

The sun was setting, a few kilometers north of the East Army a swarm of dargons gathered on a field. Not tens, not hundreds, but thousands. All the dargons gathered and faced in the same direction, to the east. Before them they bowed low with their heads firmly pressed to the ground as they prayed. They prayed to a different god then those of men and the ogres. They worshiped the dargon god, the great dragon. They did their prayers upon a mat, it was the only thing they brought with them on a campaign. A simple thatched mat made from bamboo with a dragon tattoo.

The high priest dargon stood before them with a scepter in his pincer claws. He was the only dargon clothed, and finely clothed was he. Gauzy strips of fine cloth and satin covered his exoskeleton body. He looked across the field with and nodded with admiration sweeping his scepter in an evil blessing. There were no words, not even a noise to be heard. It was silent, like death. They continued their bowing in a frenzy of religious zeal. Up and down and unrelenting.

Thomas couldn't sleep. Sleeplessness was becoming more and more usual. He carefully snuck out of the tent. The snores of many soldiers broke the silence of the still night. He wanted to see Aurella. He could easily see his way in brightly starlit sky but he had difficulty finding her tent. Every tent looked the same. In the darkness he finally found her tent, and he quietly snuck in. She wasn't awake, she slept silently like an angel with Moshki curled at her feet. He didn't wake her, he just stood for a second to look in her face and left.

Chapter 8

Nightmares in and Nightmares out

For bragging time was over and fighting time was come.

-Newbolt Henry

The Army broke camp just before the dawns break, Brax and Thomas were sore from pushups from the previous day's hazing and also for just being new privates. New Privates are always frowned upon. They went for morning breakfast, standing in line for what the other soldiers called chow.

"Chow." Brax said.

"Huh?" Thomas said.

"Chow. Funny sounding word, don't you think?"

"I can see why they don't call it food. Take a look at it." Said Thomas. "The eggs are runny, I don't what the meat is, and the bread is stale." Thomas picked up a piece of bread and hit it against a table. "Hard as steel."

"Maybe we could use it as a weapon. You know, throw it a dargon and put one of their creepy eyes out."

"You two maggots don't like my food then don't eat it." Barked a man behind the makeshift table they had set up for field rations. He was old, fat, balding and ugly.

"No sir, we shall partake of this feast." Said Brax, bowing slightly.

"Do I look like I have a sense of humor, boy?"

"No sir, not at all." Said Thomas.

"Get out of my chow line, before I run you through with your piece of bread!"

Thomas and Brax left snickering to themselves and stifling a full outburst of laughter. Eating their breakfast was worse than looking at it. But they were hungry and ate the entire meal, actually wanting more.

"Maybe we can find some nearby fruit bushes. I'll go look." Thomas said.

"I have to get back to my unit, we are supposed to drill this morning."

"Drill again?"

"Yes we march around in formation, sergeant said it will teach us discipline." Brax took a look at Thomas's open mouth look of disbelief. "I don't like it the idea of it either."

Thomas began to wonder where Jacob was, he hadn't seen him all morning.

Jacob had wondered off in the morning to forage for food, seeing what passed for army food soured his appetite and being a boy raised to hunt he knew he could find something better than mushy eggs and hard bread. Finding an apple tree nearly a mile away from the camp, he sat underneath gorging himself. He was on his fourth apple and smiling to himself thinking that the rest of the soldiers were fools for eating what they called chow. Out of nowhere three dargons appeared from across the field, they always appeared in threes it seemed to Jacob. The lifted their ugly snouts in the air smelling Jacob, nothing but large insects. Mindless and driven by hatred, they began running towards him.

Jacob nonchalantly stood, he had taken out more than just three pitiful dargons before. These three didn't even seem that big. He drew his bow and killed the first, he drew another arrow and let loose on the second. Kneeling, he easily killed the third. He went to retrieve his arrows, they were valuable, when he heard a snarling and gnashing behind him. He turned and to his horror there were many more than three. There were twenty, then more began burrowing out of the ground. With stunned disbelief he felt real fear for the first time. He began to run, knowing there was no way to take them on. The dargons gave chase, and Jacob sneaked a look over his shoulder, there were more than twenty, it was an entire army of insects.

He gave out a shout in hopes the camp could hear him. Jacob ran hard and now he regretted eating so much, his stomach churned and he stopped to throw up. He shouted again, but he was far too far from the camp still.

Aurella worked with many other women and Aurella felt much younger than all of them. Her tent was small, and luckily Aurella convinced Captain Serena to allow to just share the tent with Moshki. Moshki had curled up next to her in the middle of the night. Moshki was hungry for some cheese and crackers and Aurella was just plain sleepy. Both of them ignored the sounds of the camp and continued to napping in the early morning. The other girls rose from their tents and gave the Melfling a curious look, but most just shrugged and got ready for breakfast, Aurella and Moshki were the last ones out.Aurella had collided with a dream during the night, a dream as vivid as reality, a dream in which she was lying naked next to Thomas in a field of flowers. She realized she was in love with Thomas, something the both of them didn't know they shared.

"Up, Moshki." She nudged him with her bare toe.

"Cheese." Said Moshki sleepily.

"Sleep or cheese, you can't have both."

"Someone should come up with a way. How did you sleep?"

"Very well thank you." Aurella said trying hard to hide a smile.

"I know that look. You're in love too."

"Too?"

Moshki slapped his hand to his mouth.

Aurella smiled, "It's ok Moshki, I know the way Thomas looks at me."

"I promised him I wouldn't say anything."

"When did he tell you?"

"Right after we escaped that foul dungeon. Seems like a long time ago, but it's been just a couple of days."

"I see, but we can keep it a secret between us."

"I will, mums the word. I don't blab about anything, that's my motto."

Aurella busied herself for the day, still yawning wearily she thought of love's embrace with such a young man as Thomas. She pulled on her armor and strapped on her sword, her medical pack crossed upon her shoulder. She did like the blue armor with the red cross.

Moshki did the same, except there was no armor small enough for his Melfling stature. He refused any type of weapon, but he did acquire a very nice folding tool that contained a pair of plyers, scissors, a file, and a knife. Handier than a weapon he thought, besides a sword belt would just slip off his portly belly. He acquired the handy little tool when the quartermaster wasn't looking. He kept it in his vest pocket, next to his lock pick set. "Hmm, odd I'm missing a gold coin." He said to himself.

There were the sounds of the Army mounting on the highway outside, horses neighing and rattling of stirrups, this was a strange new life she thought. Something strange, something wonderful, something maybe fearsome. In the morning's early darkness gathered a brood of Dargons. Aurella sensed them and hurried to complete her tasks. Then horns started to blow from every direction.

Captain Serena yelled at her. "Time to earn your keep, princess. A battle is starting."

Grabbing her lute, Aurella ran outside, with Moshki beside her trying to keep up. There was an eerie silence, the horns had stopped. Aurella watched as men began to form up in a line behind an ancient rock wall as tall as a man. She stayed her ground, and began to play a battle song on her lute. She desperately wondered where her brother and Thomas were. The song was upbeat and she began to play with a fierce intensity. With horror she watched as dargons began leaping over the wall, she slung her lute over her shoulder and pulled out the medical bag running to the wall to give aid.

Moshki shook his head, "This is bad, very bad." But he ran beside her, knowing of nothing better to do at that moment. He knew that his best chances were sticking with her.

"Do you know how to use that sword?" Moshki yelled.

"No, not at all."

"Not very comforting at this moment, m'lady."

"Sorry, I play music. I think I can figure out the sword if need it, there aren't that many moving parts to it."

Aurella rushed to a wounded man, she and Moshki pulled him back away from the wall and began bandaging his wounds. She applied some of herbs to draw out the poison.

Moshki saw a dargon coming, and pushed Aurella out of the way just as it almost jumped on her. The dargon tumbled away and rolled, turning around it gnashed its teeth and gave out a barking sound. It began charging back at the two, but Aurella pulled out her sword and held it out, as leapt on her again. The dargon impaled itself on her sword and it fell twitching to the ground. Aurella gave it another swing and the twitching stopped.

"I guess you can use the sword." Gasped Moshki, staring at the dargon.

"I didn't have time to think. You saved my life."

"You can return the favor later."

The man she had treated was now lying dead on the ground. His armor shredded at his shoulder where the dargon had torn through his armor, a pale blank expression now settled on his face.

Serena had seen what was gathering on the hill and ordered her people to gather in line. "Forward!" She cried, with a tear in her eye. "We may die now, we may die later, the end is always the same, but I will not die a coward."

They all rushed forward, and die they did. They died in horrible fashions, torn to shreds and succumbing to the poison.

Aurella and Moshki stayed together, going about the battlefield treating the wounded. What few wounded there were, most lay dead or beyond care and soon would join the dead. Still searching desperately for their friends. The battle was over, humans were the victors that day, but it seemed a shallow win. There were so few survivors, mostly the men and women of the Templars who were in the rear treating the wounded. Captain Serena, however, had gathered many of the Templars together to lead the final charge and win the day. She was wounded and now lay dying. Aurella was treating her with last of the medical supplies she possessed. Her face was gray and shallow, but her beauty still held. Her armor was no longer a shiny blue, it was now bloodied and dented.

"Don't bother, child."

"I'll keep trying. You're not gone yet." Said Aurella. "No disrespect to your orders ma'am."

Serena fell back, and rested her head. Relaxing her body as death began to take her.

"Are you a Godly girl Aurella?"

"No ma'am."

"Most of the Templars are god fearing. Do you believe in God?"

"I don't know."

"You don't know? It should be one or the other, there's not really an in between."

"I guess I've never really gave it much thought."

"Give it some thought." Serena said with a smile. "I know there is something on the other side of this life for me. That's why I'm not trembling with fear for my death."

"Let me sing you a song."

In the hearts of boys and men,

Lies the ravages of sin,

But all is not lost,

All is not gone,

Hope is there for but at a cost,

Forgive and forget all the wrong.

"I thought you weren't religious?" Serena asked?

"I learned it from my mother, I didn't know it was a religious song."

"I've never heard it before, but forgiveness is a godly value. One of the biggest."

Those were Serena's last words. She passed away despite the song, but Aurella knew that sometimes in the best of songs could not heal all wounds. She wondered about her words, a Godly song. She had never given it much thought to the meanings of her songs, she sang them in hopes they would do their work.

Two hours earlier, Horns started blowing to alert the Army of the East, men all young and old, women and young girls readied for war. A battle was about to begin. Thomas reached for his bow and sword and hurried for protection behind a stone wall along with many others. A lieutenant yelled at Thomas to take the left side where there was an opening in the wall. It was cold and Thomas's heart was racing, his fast paced breathing could be seen with frosty presence. Calm down he thought, calm down. Looking up, he saw three ravens hanging from a tree, upside down by some string. They were dead, and twisted at their necks. What it meant, he didn't know.

"Bad sign." Said a grizzled man beside him.

"What's that?" asked Thomas.

"Three ravens. Bad sign."

Suddenly two dargons appeared and without thinking he took them down with two arrows, shooting as fast as any had there had ever seen.

"Welcome to the war!" said a young boy. Thomas didn't know his name and never would. A dargon jumped over the wall ripping his throat, Thomas grabbed his knife and stabbed it to death. He was now covered in both human and dargon blood. The dargon blood was as black as a moonless night. He chanced a look over the wall and he shot four more with his arrows, one refused to go down and leapt on him sending Thomas to the ground and pinning him. Thankfully, a man next to him killed it with an axe and pulled the dargon off of him.

As he pulled the dargon off Thomas, another gripped the man's throat that had saved Thomas not a second before and killed him. Thomas killed that one with his knife as well, stabbing it twice, and it was then he realized the dargons were everywhere. Dead men lay all around him and he stood alone.

"Hold the line!" he heard someone yell.

"Where was the line?" Was all Thomas could think. He understood perfectly the line wasn't where he was standing at the moment. He picked up his sword and his bow and began running to human contact, meeting with a group of stragglers desperately fighting off a small group of dargons.

A troop of men in armor and armed with swords burst their way through the right flank. They slashed their way through the brood of dargons and the soldiers around them began to cheer. The armored soldiers began pushing the brood back, pushing them up a knoll. The men's encouragement quickly changed. On the hill appeared a dargon, well not quite a dargon, it was different. It was much larger than the rest with it one claw that it snapped up above its head feverishly. However, it wasn't using the claw, it seemed to be controlling the movements of the lesser dargons. What happened next was most horrible. Hundreds of Goblins appeared on the battlefield, they were in league with the dargons. Armed with bows, the Goblins let loose their arrows. The dargons went into a frenzy and more came leaping from in back of the hill. The humans were now losing the battle. Thomas saw Brax in the middle of the hill and he rushed to help him.

A demon fell from the sky, a fat winged demon as round as a ball. His body was black with red stripes with oddly small legs and arms protruding out almost comically.His name was Baazal. Baazal was time thief, a dirty little time thief and he stole it from people who needed it most. He stole time with purpose and without remorse. Bazaal was stupid and dimwitted, but in his lacking he made up for by being devious. He didn't hold sides; he didn't care which side won. He was completely neutral and he was only there for his own amusement. An evil wizard from the south requested that he go to the battle but he would have showed up anyway, he enjoyed his work. For Thomas everything turned into slow motion, he ran but he felt like he was hardly moving.

The specter of death appeared as well, he walked the battlefield taking the souls of men. Death was dressed in a colorful robe as he gathered up the souls in great earthen vase on his back. He left the dargons alone for they had no soul. Death and the time thief often worked together but they were not friends. Baazal flew by him but Death paid him no heed.

Hundreds of dargons began swarming the hill like a pestilence, men were being shredded by their bites and their screams of agony began filling the air. Thomas slew a hundred until he ran out of arrows, but he could not reach Brax and he stood in horror as his friend was torn apart and killed. He watched helplessly as Brax fell to the ground.

Thomas fell to his knees when a dargon grabbed and pushed him to the ground, he pulled his knife and stabbed it twice as it collapsed upon him. This proved to save him however because the swarm began to pass him by but he could hardly breathe.Blood began to soak the ground, both dargon and human, the dargon blood was foul and black as midnight. Baazal flew down to the ground and landed a few feet from Thomas. He looked at Thomas and gave a slight giggle.

"Nightmares in and nightmares out, that's business." Said Baazal with indifference. Thoughts became a blur and Thomas fell into unconsciousness and the nightmares came with a force. They were disjointed dreams that made little sense, small rat like creatures nibbled at his toes, a bearded man tried to stab him, he spun wildly around, but his worst dream was his mother's ghost staring at him from the grave. Bazaal was the demon in charge of nightmares, and he did as he was told to do.

Aurella and Moshki went from body to body looking for their friends. It was Moshki who would find Thomas first, he was able to because of his short stature and was able to make out Thomas face from beneath a dead dargon.

"Aurella come here, I think it's Thomas!" Moshki shouted.

Aurella felt trepidation, her greatest fear was that Thomas had been slain. Moshki and Aurella tried to heave the body off of Thomas and with great relief to Aurella, he let out a slight moan. With all the strength they could muster they heaved again and was able to get the carcass off of him. Thomas was badly bruised and beaten with scratches and gouges all over him. Aurella treated his wounds which were many but seemed like there were none that were threatening to his life. Thomas came to and was relieved to see Aurella and Moshki looking down at him.

"You're a sore sight but you'll be ok Thomas." Aurella said with a smile.

"Brax is gone." Was all that Thomas could muster to say, his sides hurt and his ribcage was badly bruised.

Aurella's smile left her face and turned to sadness. "I'm so sorry." She said. "Where is he?"

"I don't think there's anything left of him."

Moshki reached down reached down his paw and tried to comfort Thomas. A strange feeling was coming over him, he was now caring for these humans that he travelled with for so far. Thomas got up with a lot of hesitation, he hurt all over. The three of walked around looking for Jacob, he was in a field all alone, and unfortunately they found what was left of him, he was torn to pieces as well. Aurella fell to her knees and began to cry.

"What do we do now?" Moshki asked.

"We bury him."

"I mean where do we go."

"Continue to port and try and book passage to Trilliane." Thomas said.

"Aren't you afraid of desertion?" Moshki asked.

"There's nothing left to desert." Aurella said.

Thomas began looking around frantically.

"What's wrong?" asked Moshki and Aurella in unison.

"My father's sword, it's gone."

They searched frantically nearby and through the bodies of the dead to no avail. The sword that belonged to Thomas's father was gone. Thomas let his head down, to have a true friend is rare, to lose him in war was so hard that he could not face it anymore, and to have lost Jacob as well was too much. To see their torn and crushed bodies was a sight he couldn't forget.

"Brax was my best friend in the world. We knew each other since we were barely able to walk. My mother would watch him while his parents worked in their inn. We were always causing trouble for my poor mother, everything from bringing home a stray dogs or making charcoal drawings on our stone floor, which she would scold us while she mopped it up. We swore to each other even when we were young that we would run off and find adventure. We found it, but it's not what I expected. Everything is lost."

Aurella reached down and kneeled next to Thomas, she held his hands and began to cry again.

"I've lost everything, Aurella. My friends, my father and mother. I even managed to lose my father's last possessions."

"Not quite everything." Aurella knew it was small consolation but she held out his father's bag and gave it to Thomas. Moshki had found it while helping the wounded and recognized the bag, the book, gems, and gold were still in there.

"You're a poor thief, Moshki." Laughed Thomas.

"I only steal from those that deserve it," said Moshki "…and sometimes complete strangers but that's neither here nor there. I think we should get moving, this place is turning foul."

"We'll leave at night, there are still a few survivors about, and I don't want them seeing us leave." Thomas said.

Far off in a castle in Storm Gap, the capital city of the four corners, a necromancer stood in his library. He was evil and his true name was unknown but the people called him The Prince. He had no royal blood but he liked it but he had no idea why or how the name got started. He ruled the country. He ruled it from the shadows, from secrecy and through magic. The King of Storm Gap was a doddering old man who had a good heart but a feeble body, he was sick constantly and now tried to rule from his bed. To look at The Prince, you would not know he was a practitioner of the dark arts, he did not dress in fancy robes or grow his beard to ridiculous lengths like some foppish wizard. In fact, he was clean shaven, except for a rectangular patch of beard on his chin. He carried no staff, and practiced his magic unbeknownst to the rest of the peasants of Storm Gap.He wore no hat, pointed or otherwise, his long gray hair was pulled tightly back into a pony tail. His power was not just in his craft, but also in his quest for knowledge. He studied everything and collected books from the ancient days, he read vigorously about math and histories of the world. The library was not just for book storage for him, he performed conjuring, magic, and scrying from his library. It was his place of solitude.

He controlled the Order of the Hammer, and was now bothered that he had to find sufficient replacements from his losses in that dreadful dungeon.

"Fools." He said aloud and to himself. He watched the whole thing on his table, a mystical screen that stood in the middle of his library. The table let off vapors as if it was a smoldering piece of wood, however it was made of the finest black marble, and the swirling vortex of mist gave The Prince the ability to see what he needed to see. Unfortunately, he thought, it could not see the future. He watched the battle between the dargons and men unfold before his eyes, and he had giggled slightly as dargons lay waste to the land. For now, the dargons held their purpose for his final cause.

Baazal flew in a lumbering style not unlike a bumblebee, flying through The Prince's library window, with him he carried a sword twice as large as himself and he struggled with the weight. Baazal lacked any skill or aptitude, flying as if he were drunk from too much wine. He landed upon a bookshelf with all the grace of a large rock falling off a cliff, knocking off books to the floor in the process and causing a clatter.

The Prince shook his head in disbelief but was happy none the less. He sent Bazaal on a mission, and now he hoped it was complete. His table was limited in ways, and he was unable to see many things, he had missed what had become of the Kray child, Thomas.

"Do you have it?" inquired The Prince.

"Yes, of course master, it's in my hands!"

"That's a sword you idiot."

"Yes master, it's the sword of Lord Kray."

"I summoned you to plague the Kray child with nightmares and follow him around. When the Order of the Hammer was killed I tasked you to get the key. I explained to you that the key was a book."

"What's a book master? I thought a book would be some sort of weapon, so I retrieved the sword for you as bidden."

"A book is a leather bound compilation of papers with words, the book I seek is black leather, not much bigger than a man's hand. Look around you, there are hundreds of them on these shelves, and through your oafishness you knocked over some irreplaceable ones."

"So this is not a book?" asked Baazal, holding up the sword, the name of Kray was emblazoned on the base of the blade and the hilt shined like silver.

"No, that's not a book, that's a sword." The Prince grabbed it from him and tossed it on a nearby chair. "A souvenir at best." He said angrily between his teeth. "Go back out and find the Kray child and get the book." He commanded.

"Yes master." Baazal flew out with the same clumsiness he flew in with, slamming the side of a window and nearly breaking it.

Ravana knocked on her father's library door, a tray of tea and cakes in her left hand. She had heard the clatter of books from her own study, and although she was used to strange noises she still liked to check in on her father. More out of morbid curiosity than worry.

She knocked again. "Father!" she called.

Ravana was delighted as a small child, before she was hardly able to walk, her father would summon demons and the dead. She was spoiled and whenever she asked him to do it again, he would always give into her until he had exhausted his powers. He gave her diamonds and pearls and taught her in the dark ways. She had every toy imaginable, but she discarded them all and instead dabbled in witchcraft. Ravana was beautiful, she had jet black hair and soft pale skin. Her hair fell around her face in a heart shape, and a diamond necklace showed off her delicate neckline, however her soul was dreadful.Her anger and hellish temperament never brought willing suitors. She was known for throwing public tantrums when she didn't get her way. She preferred cold and cloudy days and always kept her bedroom with the curtains drawn to keep out the sun. She would sleep until the late in the morning and begin her day by yelling at the wait staff.

She lived the life of luxury but to her it was unsatisfying, this castle is too small, she would complain to her father. Her favorite place in the castle was a tall tower, five stories high, where she like to lean out and look at the passing peasants, sometimes for fun, she would spit on them. She rarely went outside in the sunlight and if she did it was in the early evening to look out over Storm Gap and look down on the people below.

She knocked again, "Father!" she called with slight impatience. She knew she shouldn't open the door without his permission.

The Prince opened the door. "What is it, Ravana?"

"I brought you tea and cakes." She smiled. "What was all the commotion in here? I heard some loud crashing noises and some gruff man talking."

"There was no gruff man in here, I summoned a minor demon to fetch a book for me. Unfortunately, he's as dumb as he is clumsy. He knocked over several books. I was just in the process of replacing them in their rightful places when you came. Thank you for the tea. Now be gone with you."

"A demon, which one? Can I play with him?"

"Bazaal, a minor demon, he's left already."

"You mentioned a book father. What's so important about a book?"

"You know how I like to collect books."

"But summoning a demon to get a book, that's a bit much even for you. You usually just buy them."

"This book is special, I just recently learned of its existence. It was supposed to have been destroyed hundreds of years ago but somehow a copy of it survived."

"And why do you want this copy so badly?"

"This book is very important; it could possibly hold the destruction of our way of life if the words of this book spreads. It holds the key men's hope and will."

"This book is dangerous then?"

"Yes very, I don't intend to keep, I plan to destroy it."

"You! Destroy a book? That doesn't sound like you at all, this must be very serious."

"It is. Now I said be gone, I have work to do."

Ravana pouted and shut the door behind her.

"Do you know how to get to Korinth Port from here?" asked Aurella.

"Raven's Port is probably closer now." Thomas said.

"How do we get there?"

"We have to head back east where we came from, then cut south through Cross Falls."

"Ummm. Cross Falls?" inquired Moshki.

"Yes, it's the shortest way now. Is that a problem?"

"No no, it will be ok. Meep." Moshki said with a gulp.

Three dead ravens in a tree." Thomas said aloud.

"Huh?" Moshki gave Thomas a puzzled look.

"Three ravens in tree. Bad sign."Now Aurella gave him a puzzled look as well, but Thomas just sat in silence.

Thomas took out the book and turned it over once more, it was black leather with gold lettering on the front. Ancient runes maybe, thought Thomas. His father had gold and jewels, why did he have this book? He didn't have it with him when he went to war. Perhaps he found it in the citadel.

They waited for nightfall which had not been far off and once again they set off on a trek, tired, but they knew they had to move on. Thomas had spent the day unconscious under a dead dargon, he was sore and bruised. He felt like an ogre had stepped on him with one large boot, then scraped him off like some sticky nuisance.

They were all tired from the battle, Moshki thought nothing more than getting into a warm bed. Maybe he would be ok if they went to Cross Falls, all melflings looked the same to humans. Being tossed out of Cross Falls was slightly humiliating in front of the cute melfling girl. Sparkling brown eyes, she had, hopefully he would find her again. Love should never be wasted, a chance for romance should not be lost.

"Warm bed, real food, cheese, and beer." Said Moshki.

"Nice words of encouragement." Smiled Aurella.

"Hot bread, butter, a slice of steak done just right." He continued.

They reached Cross Falls after midnight, they would go to bed hungry, all the lights in Cross Falls were out and there would be no one still awake to take them in or provide a meal. Thomas made a large fire, feeling safe so close to town. Aurella curled up next to Thomas.

"Keep me warm." She said.

The moon was out, and every star imaginable shown their twinkling lights. Thomas realized his hand was close to her hand, touching. He let his hand fall on the inside of hers. He took a deep breath and dared to hold her hand. She didn't stop him or pull away, she held on to his hand in return. Thomas was sleepy but his heart was beating fast. The warm glow of the fire gave off warmth, but the warmth in her heart was greater. She laid her head on his lap, and her hair fell into her face, Thomas gently brushed it away from her eyes and she smiled. Her smile, thought Thomas. Her smile could melt him. The smell of her hair, the fire flickered in eyes. A kiss? He wondered. Not yet.

"I feel safe with you, Thomas. The world is in turmoil, but I know nothing can hurt me as long as I'm with you."

Next morning Thomas awoke, Aurella was still on his lap and Moshki was curled up next to both of them. Thomas yawned and stretched disturbing both of them.

"Sorry." Said Moshki, "I got cold in the night, didn't mean to intrude on you two."

"It's alright Moshki, I think we've been through enough to get this close." Thomas laughed. "We should get to Cross Falls. Maybe stay the night, get rested, cleaned up and get some supplies."

"I know a great place, the Drunken Dragon Inn. Warm and cozy with good food and plenty of beer." Moshki said.

"Sounds good Moshki, but I don't drink beer." Said Aurella.

"That's the beauty of beer, my dear. You don't have to drink it; I'll drink it for you."

"A hot bath sounds good to me, Moshki." Said Thomas. "I still have the blood of yesterday's battle on me. Fresh clothes and a bath for me."

"I've one favor to ask, Thomas."

"What's that?"

"While we're in Cross Falls…" Moshki trailed off, and twiddling his fingers.

"Yes."

"Call Mister… Smith. Don't call me Moshki."

"And why would I do that?

"My cousin was also called Moshki and he was thrown out of Cross Falls over a bit of a misunderstanding. At least don't call me Moshki in front of other people, so they don't get confused. And if someone asks, I'm just Mister Smith, Nicolai Smith."

"No problems, Mister Smith."

"Oh, one more thing…"

"And what's that?"

"Take my vest and put it in your backpack."

Thomas gave him a puzzled look but complied with his request. Thomas was beginning think that Moshki had left Cross Falls on less than good terms.

"You look funny naked." Said Aurella to Moshki.

"Ha ha," He laughed sarcastically. Melflings' wear clothes to keep their belongings in, not because we're concerned about our wardrobes. I'm not naked, I have a beautiful coat of fur, thank you."

They walked passed a large creek, the water as wide as three lengths of men fell off a cliff, splitting in two streams and crossed in the center. The morning sun released a rainbow underneath.

"It's beautiful." Exclaimed Aurella. "Now I see why it's called Cross Falls."

"Of course, most names have meanings and reasons. Your name means a shining golden glow." Moshki said.

"What does your name mean?"

"Nothing." Said Moshki, regretting his remark. In his language his name meant rogue, and he meant to keep it a secret for now. He was beginning to like his new found friends, and didn't want to lose them if they found out he came from a family of thieves.

The children of Cross Falls came out to look at the strange sight, two young foreigners traveling with a melfling. An odd curiosity, Cross Falls had more and more people passing through. An overgrown mouse was nothing new, but a melfling with humans was odd. The children ran up to them and ran around them playfully.

"Do you have any copper?" A little girl asked Thomas.

"Shoo!" Moshki chided her.

"It's ok, Mister Smith." Said Thomas remembering his odd request. Thomas reached into his pocket and threw pennies up in the air. The children laughed and scrambled for the pennies. One boy, dressed in rags, noticed Aurella's lute.

"Play us song." He said.

"Yes please!" They all shouted.

They jumped for joy when she pulled the lute from off her back and she began to play.

Aurella's Song

I sat upon on a hill, sipping a cup of tea
Across the far off horizon, I surveyed the sea
A ship sailed in from origins unknown
Brave eagles upon the rock have flown.

Shadows fell in length across the grassy hill
A tree bristled and lamented, 'I cannot tolerate this chill,
I want to move to warmer climes
But I'm not as nimble as in earlier times'.

Bowing to the stately elm, I said 'hello'
I took off my cloak and wrapped it around his bough.

'You are too kind,' he said, 'to such the likes of me,
I have no money or gift that I could give to thee'.

Then said I, 'I'd rather have friends, than silver or gold,
I'd rather have love, then riches untold.
I'd rather have friends, then to be the queen of a mountain top.'
'Please, consider when I am but a memory
And I am buried beneath
Wrap your roots around and please return the warmth.'
Then I sang happy tune and tumbled down the hill
Rambling to another land, it seemed as time stood still.
I hopped aboard that sailing ship, vowing to someday return
I will miss this place, but my heart it seems to yearn.

A robin lit upon the mast and sang along with me
Traveling forth without a care, she said, is truly being free
Said I, 'to Trilliane I wander, to sing a new song,
For I am told that in that land, one can do no wrong.'

Smiling to the robin and reaching into my pack
I gave the little bird to eat a bit of hard tack.

'You are too kind,' she said, 'to such the likes of me,
I have no money or gift that I could give to thee'.

Then said I, 'I'd rather have friends, than silver or gold,
I'd rather have love, then riches untold.
I'd rather have friends, then to be the queen of a mountain top.'

'Please, consider when I am but a memory
And buried upon the hill.
Alight upon the elm, and please return the song.'
I sat upon the helm and watched the robin soar
I turned my head and saw the distant shore
My destiny uncertain, my fate is unknown
I sing for now but time will tell to see what will be shown.

The children were all mesmerized by Aurella's song at first, but then they all began to cheer. Thomas had been mesmerized as well, and just sat back and enjoyed Aurella's beauty and the way she bit her lip when she looked back at Thomas. He loved her red hair and the way it cascaded around her face, he loved her smile and he loved her smooth skin. He loved her voice and her eyes. He loved everything about her. The girls in his village seemed so far off now, and he never remembered looking at a girl the way he looked at Aurella.

"There it is!" Exclaimed Moshki. "The Drunken Dragon Inn, warm bed and food for us!"

"Hot bath!" Said Aurella.

"Steak!" Said Thomas.

"I'm buying." Said Moshki.

Thomas and Aurella looked at him a little surprised.

"It's the least I can do; you've done so much for me."

"We owe you." Said Aurella, "Without you we would have never made it out of the dungeon, and you saved my life from that dargon."

"Ah, but you became my friends, that's something better."

They entered the Drunken Dragon and sat in a corner. It was a seedy looking place with all likes of people from far away eating and drinking. Dark looking men from far off places, a mage sat in another corner, his head in his hands. A waitress quickly came to take their order, eyeing Moshki suspiciously.

"Odd looking people here, I've never seen the likes." Said Aurella. "There is a strange looking creature with the head of a fish, and he has tentacles!"

"Quit staring, m'lady." Moshki said. "There are some rough men here, mercenaries, assassins and refugees."

"There's another man with four arms, scary!"

"You guys order first." Moshki offered.

"I'll have a steak." Said Thomas.

"Me too." Said Aurella.

"I'll have a steak, with mushrooms and a baked potato. Also I would like a side order of coleslaw. I side order of beans. I side order of ham. Oh, and some cheese, a wedge of cheese, the stinkiest cheese you have, please."

"Is that all?" She eyed him up and down.

"Do you have bacon?"

"Yes!"

"Is there a problem miss?" Aurella asked.

"We've had a few melflings come through here, always trouble. Strange I've never seen one travelling with humans before." The waitress nearly barked.

"This one is no problem, miss." Interjected Thomas. "He's an upstanding citizen and I'll vouch for him."

"We ran one out of town not two days ago for thieving, he had a strange name I don't remember it."

"Well this is Mister Smith, He's been with us for weeks now." Said Thomas.

The waitress gave a hurumph sound and walked back with their orders.

"I forgot the beer." Said Moshki.

"Thieving, Moshki?"

"Sorry it's what I do, melflings have a hard time finding regular work." He said apologetically.

They finished their meal ravenously because they hadn't had a decent meal in days. Moshki finished two beers and his enormous meal.

"Burp." Was the only thing he could manage.

"We should get rooms." Said Thomas.

"I have no money."

"Don't worry, I'll get yours. I have enough."

"Just take out a little gold Thomas, if you flash all your money it will attract unwanted attention."

Thomas heeded Moshki's advice and took out a couple of coins. "Do you think this enough?" Asked Thomas to Moshki.

"And then some, make sure you get change."

Thomas went to the innkeeper. "I would like two rooms for the night, sir."

The innkeeper was a round man with a stubbly face. "Only one room, left. Lots of people coming through on their way to Raven's Port to escape this cursed land. I may be leaving soon myself." The man was more jovial then he looked. "The room only has two beds, but I can't let you have it, you being with that girl there, boy and a girl together, unless you're brother and sister."

"Oh we're married." Chimed in Aurella. "And this is Mister Smith." She said looking at Moshki.

"You're married? So young, what's the world coming to?" He shook his head. "Is that melfling with you?"

"Yes sir."

"Mind you keep him in check. We've had trouble with their lot recently."

Moshki heard him but was relieved that he wasn't recognized. The innkeeper had taken rent from him many times during his stay at Cross Falls.

"Here's the key." Thomas gave him a gold piece in the man quickly put it in his pocket.

"Change please." Said Moshki, in commanding voice that surprised both Thomas and the innkeeper.

The innkeeper gave Moshki an evil eye but reached into his register and gave Thomas a few pieces of silver.

Ulysses raised his head up from his hands. He had started drinking early, whiskey. No one in this place blinked twice about his early morning drinking. He was now sloshed and recognized the boy Thomas Kray instantly. He was drunk but his perceptions were still intact, but he did not care. He and Borgman had a falling out after the dungeon incident, the Order of the Hammer was nearly wiped out and Borgman had blamed Ulysses for his own ineptitude. Borgman went back to Storm Gap to regroup and get more men. Ulysses had had enough and decided it was time to start self-employment. He didn't care if he worked cheap magic shows for fun, he was no one's lack or scapegoat. He got up and paid his tab. He would travel to Raven's Port to book passage as well.

Aurella, Thomas and Moshki spent the rest of the day going about the town. Thomas bought food and fresh clothing for him and Aurella, Moshki bought himself another vest and even a pair of sharp blue pants to make himself look different. Melflings rarely wore pants, he was a little bothered that the only pair that fit him were from the children's section. They were baggy and he rather liked the way they looked in the mirror.

They spent the night in peace, in a room that wasn't heated but the beds were comfortable. Moshki slept at the foot of Aurella curled up in a ball. Aurella lay awake and wondered why Thomas hadn't kissed her the night before. Boys! She thought, what did she have to do to get his attention?

Baazal lumbered through the night trying to pick up the scent of Thomas from where he had left him, underneath the carcass of a dargon. He picked it up, using his nose like some kind of foul flying demonic bloodhound. Thomas slept peacefully in a nightmare free slumber. Instead he dreamt of Aurella, touching her, holding her, kissing her.

Chapter 9

The Pale Witch

"The time has come," The Walrus said, "To talk of many things: Of shoes – and ships – and sealing wax - Of cabbages – and kings – And why the sea is boiling hot – And whether pigs have wings."

-Lewis Carroll

Borgman walked into the castle of The Prince, he had a long journey behind him and was unaccustomed to travelling without a mount. He was tired but this was his first stop before he would go to his home and hopefully get some much needed rest. He was soldier and used to being outside, but now he was older and a comfortable bed, warm fire and brandy was more his style. Sleeping on the ground and in the cold was for younger soldiers.

He waited impatiently in the hallway after notifying The Prince's servants of his arrival. The Prince came down his stairwell with grace. Borgman looked up at him, The Prince was noble looking, but that was as close to royalty as he really was. He was tall and gray haired, but the patch of beard on his chin bothered Borgman for some reason. It made him look pretentious, he thought. The black tight fitting clothes he was now wearing only added to his pretentiousness. Ravana was at the top of the stairs looking down at him, she looked smug he thought. She always had an air of contempt about her, but when Borgman saw her, he saw something that was disturbing. He just couldn't put his finger on it.

The Prince stopped midway coming downstairs and took pause looking at Borgman. "Come up stairs to my inner chamber." The Prince commanded.

"Yes my Prince."

"Where is Ulysses?"

"We parted ways." Borgman was puzzled as to why The Prince had not inquired about the others. "We lost the boy, sir. The Order of the Hammer under my rule were killed in a dungeon. By the dead. Ulysses and I barely made it out."

"I know about your ordeal. Gruesome events."

Now Borgman was even more troubled as to The Prince's knowledge. It was if he was omnipotent. "I've come for more men and to regroup some members of the Order of the Hammer."

"Why did you let Ulysses go? Not very much like you to just let a deserter free. You're slipping Borgman."

Borgman swallowed hard. He was now becoming nervous. They entered the Prince's library. Borgman was not a man of reading, total disdain for it as a matter of fact. Only the rich and well educated read.

"Ulysses slipped out just after I fell asleep, we had an argument beforehand about what we should do, and he expressed his desire to leave The Order. I resisted the urge to strike him. He's not the strongest mage around but who knows what evil craft he could conjure on me. In fact, I believe he probably cast a sleep spell upon me so as I would not wake when he left. In the morning he was gone."

"I see. Very prudent. Probably the best thing coming back here to get more men instead of striking off on your own to take out a boy."

Borgman cringed at the loaded barb. "We completely lost him in the dungeon, sir. No sign of him, and if I had pursued him further I would be dead as well."

"Totally understandable. I meant what I said, relax Borgman. You are being jumpy; you need to get your sense of humor back. Come let me pour you a drink."

The Prince poured Borgman a drink of brandy into a fine glass, pouring himself one as well. Borgman drank it in one shot, but The Prince savored his, smelling it first, swirling it around in his glass and just taking a small sip.

"Here, have another." The Prince poured him a larger amount this time.

"Thank you, sir. The drink settled me down, sorry I'm so rattled."

"Follow me." The Prince moved a carpet and lifted up a door that led to a staircase going down through the floor. "I want to show you something, and this is to be kept in absolute secrecy. Do you understand?"

"Of course."

They walked down the stone steps for quite some time and Borgman realized they must be well underground.

"Do you know my real name?"

"No, sir. I know of no one that knows your true name. You've been The Prince for as long as anyone remembers." Borgman took pause at that statement and realized that he had known The Prince since he was a young man, yet The Prince appeared no older than when he was in his twenties.

"My name is Zahar."

"A magnificent and powerful name, sir."

"I wasn't looking for your approval; I'm telling you because I consider us friends… confidants. We're friends and you didn't even know my name. It occurred to me that it was wrong never to have told you. We've been to parties, got drunk together and I have never told you my name. Remember the old days when we used to go to bars?"

"Of course I do sir."

"Call me Zahar."

"Zahar, of course."

"Those were the days. You helped me through my life when my wife died. We had so much fun."

They reached the bottom of the stairs, and entered a stone chamber, a chain hung from the ceiling and there was a pit in the middle of the room. Borgman dared a glance, there was fire down below. An etching of a dragon leered menacingly back at him.

"Do you know what a necromancer is, Borgman?"

"No, Zahar." Borgman said his name this time but it tripped out of his mouth like an awkward brick.

"A necromancer is someone who summons the dead and demons. It's my true profession."

"Is there much money in that, Zahar?"

The Prince was taken aback by the question, but did not show it in his face or otherwise. He knew that Borgman was a tad stupid but the question belied reasoning.

"No I don't make money raising the dead. I use divination for making money. Seeing events and knowing where to be at that right time, the right thing to invest in."

"I see."

The Prince grew tired of the conversations. "Bound." He said in a commanding voice.

"Huh?"

"Your hands. Look. Your hands are bound." He said with a chuckle.

Borgman tried to look at his hands but he couldn't. His hands were now tied behind him. He was now in a bit of a stupor from the alcohol. He tried to think straight but couldn't. He had only two drinks and was now unable to function. He had ten times more than that before in evenings and was able to fight in combat. He tried to put his palm to his forehead to think, forgetting his wrists were unmovable.

"Your legs are bound as well." Said Zahar.

Borgman looked down helplessly at his now bound legs, wondering and unable to comprehend.

"Gaap, time to come out and play."

A beast, human in form, but with leathered wings like a bat came out of the darkness. His beard was black, black as burned charcoal. His skin was charred and thick, as if he had he had been in smoky room and the soot had clung to his body. His ears were as large as his head and two spikes protruded out of his skull out of the corners of his forehead. There was a tattoo on his right chest, a symbol of a circle in red with bold runes of a forgotten tongue. Borgman blinked his eyes hard still unable to think. His tongue was becoming thick in his mouth.

"Borgman, meet Gaap. Gaap, meet Borgman." Zahar chuckled at his own joke. "Borgman, this is my city, my kingdom, I run this place. The capital of Storm Gap got its name from me, I named it. I named it after this fellow here. I've been here awhile, a long time. I know your mistakes. You lied about Ulysses, I know you just let him go. It's ok, you were scared of his magic. But you failed in getting the boy, and instead of pursuing him while his trail was hot, you preferred to trot back home for a warm bed and getting drunk. You're old, you've outlived your usefulness."

Borgman fell to his knees staring at the demon in front of him. He could only manage to weep.

"Very unfitting, I thought you would go out fighting like the old salty dog you say are, or were I should say. Instead you're going out with a whimper."

Zahar nodded at Gaap. "Eat."

Borgman's scream stopped short as Gaap opened his large mouth and with one bite took off his head to his shoulders. His body fell limp to the floor. Zahar turned and started walking up the stairs as Gaap chewed.

Without turning The Prince said, "Enjoy."

Back in his library The Prince poured himself another drink. He took out some blue powder and laid a fine line of it on his scrying table. Taking his knife from his side, he pushed the powder into a fine line and snorted it through a glass tube. He sniffed and turned a little red. ood times he thought. He leaned back in his leather chair as he let the drug take effect.

"Aurella." Thomas whispered.

Moshki was snoring peacefully in his sleep, probably dreaming of food.

"Yes." She said.

"I can't sleep."

"Me either. And I'm cold."

"Do you want me to warm you up?"

"We are married." She said jokingly.

Aurella slipped out of bed and into Thomas's bed and under his covers. They began to kiss, passionately. There was no holding back now, the flood gates were opened. The moonlight lit the room dimly through the only window. She looked into his eyes and he in hers and they felt as one. She had slipped her pants off earlier for comfort and he felt her naked waist against his. He slipped off her blouse, and felt her naked breasts. Aurella unbuttoned Thomas's pants and slipped them off in an awkward struggle and they tried to keep quiet, giggling at their clumsiness. She took off his shirt, slowly unbuttoning it as she kissed his chest. He slid his hand up her soft thigh. He moved on top of her, and he never felt more like man than he did at that moment. Their first real kiss quickly turned to making love.

The next morning, they started off. It was a long walk to Raven's Port. Their packs slung on their backs and all very rested. They were all in an excellent mood, Thomas and Aurella couldn't help it, they would sneak smiling glances at each other as they walked along. Moshki was happy for them that they finally overcame the shyness that human love suffers from.

"Glad I'm not human." He said aloud.

"How did you sleep last night?" Aurella asked Thomas.

"I slept very well after, well you know."

"I know."

"I didn't have any nightmares."

"Nightmares?"

"Ever since my mother and father were killed, I've had these crazy nightmares."

"Like what?"

"Horrible dreams, I dreamt that a dargon was gnawing at my toes, one time. Another this great dragon came out of the mist, trying to devour me. I woke up before he did."

"They say if you die in dreams, you die in real life." Aurella said.

"I hope that's not true, I've come close several times it seems. Aurella?" Thomas trailed off in his question.

"What is it?"

"I want you to know, I really like you."

She laughed. "I really like you, too. Have you ever been with a girl before?"

"No. I was always too shy."

"I've never been with a boy either."

"When I said, I really like you, I mean I really like you a lot. I think..." He stammered. "I think I love you."

"You think... hmm. Well when you know tell me about it." She trotted up ahead to catch up with Moshki.

"Oy, I'm Glad I'm not a human." Moshki said, this time slapping the palm of his paw to his forehead.

They arrived in Raven's Port late in the afternoon. It was just like Aurella's song, they were on top of hill, and there were sparrows flying around.

"It's amazing." Aurella said. Down below in the bay there were about twenty sailing ships, big and small. Some fishing boats and the town was busy with people. They strolled into town looking at everything and everyone. It was a melting pot of people and creatures. On every corner there was a stand of vegetables, a vendor cooking food, or an old lady selling trinkets. On one corner there was a Melfling shuffling cards. He would shuffle three cards and ask a person to guess where the ace of hearts was. Thomas was fascinated by the game because a man was winning.

Moshki saw the look in his eye. "Don't even think about playing."

"Why not?"

"I know this trick, I used to do it myself. Watch."

Moshki was right, the man bet all of his money and lost it all.

"Thanks Moshki, you're a good friend."

"I would love to go shopping." Aurella said.

"Let's go."

Everywhere there were flowers and trinkets, clothes and fruits, there was too much to take in. Thomas bought Aurella another shirt and himself one too. They found themselves close to the docks and they began looking at the ships. One kiosk was deep frying some kind of food so they wandered up to the smell of cooking. He was deep frying scorpions.

"I dare you." Said Aurella.

"Dare me to what?"

"Eat one, just one…. I dare you."

Thomas looked at the deep battered scorpions that were skewered on a stick with a crinkle in his nose.

"I'll take one. Just one." He said to the vendor.

Thomas took the browned little delicacy from the vendor, staring at it and trying his best to work up his nerve. He closed his eyes and took a bite.

"Well?"

"It tastes like copper. A little bit of a peanut taste. It's like eating a nutty penny."

Aurella laughed. Thomas loved her laugh and he laughed with her. He finished his scorpion. "I dare you."

"Who me… I'm not crazy." She rolled her eyes and walked away.

"Women." Said Moshki.

Thomas nodded at Moshki. "We need to check on getting a ship for passage." Said Thomas.

"I think our best bet is to find a smaller ship, one that's not so expensive. We'll need money when we get to Trilliane." Said Moshki.

"Agreed."

They walked along the docks, inspecting the vessels.

"This one looks sturdy." Said Aurella.

"Nice choice." Moshki said. "Wide berth, it should have nice beds. It's made for passengers and also smuggling."

"How much will it cost for the three of us?" Asked Thomas of Moshki.

Moshki scratched his chin, about five, maybe no more than ten gold pieces to get to Trilliane."

A man was tying ropes near the top of the plank and Thomas approached him, daring to go up on the ship. Seafarers could be a rough bunch.

"Careful Thomas." Aurella called after him.

"Excuse me sir, we would like to book passage to Trilliane."

The man was rail thin and wore a blue and white striped shirt. He looked Thomas up and down but smiled a toothless grin at him. "We're heading there, third stop. Go see Captain Dmitry."

Pleased that he wasn't knocked over the head and robbed, Thomas became more confident. "Where can I find him?"

"Right there on the quarterdeck." He nodded his in the direction. "Wearing the long blue jacket with the gold stuff on his shoulders. Go on boy he won't hurt you."

"Are you Captain Dmitry?"

"I be."

"Sir, I'd like to book passage for me and my friends to Trilliane." He boldly said.

Captain Dmitry was a small man, shorter than Thomas but he had a large belly and full black beard. On his head was tri-corn blue hat, and he wore a blue waistcoat, he was a typical seafaring captain.

"How much do you have?"

"I've six gold pieces."

"Not enough boy. Lots of people going to Trilliane and willing to pay more."

"How much would it take?"

"Ten. Not a penny less."

"One of my friends is a melfling, he doesn't take up much space."

"He takes a full bed, and that's what yer buying."

"The melfling usually sleeps with one of us."

"They eat their weight in food and down more rum than my first mate can."

"Nine gold for the three of us. Please sir."

"Fine, nine gold it is, and ye get two berths, sharing a bed with a melfling it is, I'd be more feared of catching a fever. If there's any thieving on the ship, I'll blame the melfling first."

"Yes sir, I'll keep him check." Said Thomas.

"We sail in the morning, first light, don't be late."

"Can we stay on the ship tonight? We're tired and travelled all day."

"Yer pushing it boy, but that's ok. You can stay on the ship. Mind you my boys will be doing a lot of drinking in port tonight. Don't bother them, just stay in your berths.

"Yes sir."

"For your own safety mind you. Yer a bargainer, I like that. Welcome aboard the Pale Witch." He shook Thomas's hand heartily and gave a boisterous laugh. "Now bring your mates aboard, I'll show y'all around and explain the rules to ye."

Thomas motioned Moshki and Aurella to come aboard.

"You didn't mention the other friend was a girl."

"Is that a problem?"

"No problem, but yer in charge of her safety. That's rule number one for you."

"Yes sir, my pleasure."

"We're married." Said Aurella.

Captain Dmitry looked at her. "Don't lie to me lass, I know human nature better than any man alive, but I don't care two coppers, I'm not one to judge what one does. The life I live is not one of a saint, or any church approves of."

"Rule number two, no thieving." He looked straight at the melfling, but Moshki just gave him a 'what who me' look. "Part of rule two is no lying. Rule number three, you help with the work. Swabbing decks and general maintenance, a little work never killed anyone. Rule four, respect my crew. Rule five…" Captain Dmitry scratched his bearded chin for a minute and looked as if he was making up the rules on the spot. "I don't have a rule five yet, but if'n I do think of one you'd best adhere to it. Yer a rot sorry look'n lot."

Captain Dmitry showed them around the ship. "The front of the ship is called the bow, the rear is aft, or stern. The right side as yer facing the bow is the starboard side, the left is port. This side is always starboard, don't get yer right hand mixed up with which side is starboard and which side is port."

"I like this guy," whispered Aurella in Thomas's ear, "much nicer than that Sergeant Major. He hasn't told us to shut our pie holes."

Thomas laughed, "You're funny."

The Captain showed them to their berthing room. It was small two beds, one on top of the other, barely enough room to stand and change in. "This your room. Be on deck at sunrise tomorrow when we set sail."

They went back to shore to eat dinner; the scorpion was not quite enough to fill Thomas's appetite. There were scores of seafood restaurants lined all along the docks. Neither Thomas nor Aurella had ever had seafood and as it seems, Thomas would eat anything, especially if he was dared. Moshki ordered crab and Thomas ordered a lobster. Aurella preferred normal food and kept with ordering a steak.

"You and bugs." Said Aurella.

"This isn't a bug, it's a lobster."

"It's a sea bug, not much different than that scorpion you ate earlier."

"This tastes better."

"It looks like too much work."

They finished their meals, and this time Moshki didn't forget his beer. Thomas drank a couple as well and they all felt very good.

Aurella drank some wine, and after only half a glass she was giggling and tipsy.

"Nap time." Said Moshki.

"Agreed." Said Aurella.

"I'm going to go back into town, there's something I want to get." Thomas said.

"You know how to get back here?" Asked Aurella.

"I never get lost. I'll be back soon."

Aurella and Moshki returned their berth, Moshki crawled up and plopped down on the top bunk. Aurella took the bottom bunk. Moshki began to snore but Aurella just laid there with her eyes closed. She wondered what the heck Thomas went for all by himself. Later, Moshki left the room to smoke his pipe on the deck. Thomas returned to the room after only a short time later and opened the door quietly. Aurella opened her eyes and looked at him, leaning on one elbow. Thomas looked back at her and smiled.

"I know that I love you."

"You do, do you, and how do you know you love me."

"Because you're the first thing I think about when I wake up in the morning. You're the last thing I think about before I fall asleep. You pervade my dreams. You make laugh, and just thinking of you puts a smile on my face. I love your hair and the way you smell. I love the way you smile, and the way you bite your lip. When I'm with you my heart soars, and I never want the time we're together to end. The kiss of your lips is sweeter than anything I have ever tasted. I'm sorry I have butterflies in my stomach just working up the nerve to tell you these words."

"I went back into town to get you this…" Thomas reached out and gave her a single red rose.

"I love you too, Thomas. Why were you so afraid to tell me?"

"I was afraid of so many things, the wrong time after all that has happened to us. It was too soon; we've only known each other for a week. I was afraid you wouldn't love me in return. All these things just rolled around in my head, but I'm not scared of that anymore. I'm with you."

"Well I love you, I think I loved you the first day I saw you."

Aurella stood up, and Thomas pulled her to him. He cupped her face and stroked her cheek, he kissed her more passionately than ever before. She wrapped her arms around his neck and kissed him back. She began to tremble, he kissed her harder. He slid his hand up her waist and caressed her hips and squeezed her tight. He slipped her blouse off and kissed her breasts and they tumbled into bed. Their passion was uncontrollable. She slipped his pants off and began to kiss him at his waist. Aurella began to moan, and they made love again. And again.

Moshki returned shortly after dark and saw the two humans curled up on the bottom bunk. Jealous of not being able to snuggle with Aurella this night, he crawled to the top bunk and slept alone.

The next morning, they were on the deck, the sun was rising over the bay and it was such a sight to see. There was an intense excitement of finally setting sail as the men were busy casting off ropes and pushing off the dock. The sails were raised, and the men began singing a song.

Shove off ye matey,
Pull up the ropes ye matey,
Aweigh the anchor ye matey,

We've a long sail ahead,
Till we can go to bed,

Hoist the sails ye matey,
Trim the rudder ye matey,
Batten the hatches ye matey,
We've a long sail ahead,
Till we can go to bed,

She's a lovely girl ye matey,
Wave goodbye ye matey,
Blow your kisses ye matey,
We've a long sail ahead,
Till we can go to bed.

The three of them stood feeling somewhat in the way of things as the hearty looking sailors busied themselves, but that moment was short lived. The Captain strolled up to them with his hands on his hips and a hearty laugh.

"Time for your jobs."

"We're paying customers." Said Moshki.

"I don't want y'as to feel out of place. What's yer name boy?"

"Thomas, sir."

"And yours lassie?"

"Aurella." She didn't like being called lassie and she showed red.

"You both get to clean my cabin. Easy work, don't worry, I'm not gonna have you doing anything dangerous. Ok, now for you melfling."

"The name's Moshki, thank you."

"Moshki, see that crow's nest up that mast?"

"You mean that thing made of wood, that looks like it will fall apart."

"That's it. Climb yourself up there, you get to be the lookout."

"Lookout for what?"

"Other ships and sech."

"What other ships?" Moshki suddenly became worried.

"Any ships flying the skull and cross bone flag, or even worse, the flag of the Federation."

"And why would we have to worry about federation ships? Asked Aurella.

"We may be carrying a little extra load; if'n you know what I mean. We have to avoid the authorities as well as pirates. Tis a smuggler's struggle"

"Rum." Said Moshki.

"And you'll keep your little paws out of it, my men don't even get to drink it. It's under lock and key anyway."

Like a lock is going to stop me, thought Moshki.

"Bring plenty of water with you, Moshki." Captain Dmitry said. "Gets mighty hot up there, don't want you falling out from the dehydration. Keep your eyes open, we'll be pulling into Storm Gap in the morning before sunrise. Federation ships will be all around. Drinking is illegal there, we make a good bit of gold every haul."

Moshki grabbed some water, and climbed the mast to the crow's nest. Being a lookout seemed an easy enough job but Moshki grumbled curse words in the melfling tongue all the way up anyway. Aurella and Thomas cleaned the Captain's cabin as he told them. It wasn't hard, Thomas made the bed and Aurella dusted. The Captain came in and they thought they would be in trouble because they were also goofing around a little. The Captain looked around approvingly though. They had both been amazed at how nice the cabin was.

"Nice job. Thomas, do you play chess?"

"No sir."

"It's the game of kings."

"My father played, it always seemed so complicated."

"Do you know the moves then?"

"I do."

"Let us play then. The men on this ship don't play, except my first mate. He's a sore loser though."

Thomas lost five games in row as Aurella watched.

"Yer not a bad player, Thomas. But yer afraid to lose a piece. As a Captain, you have to be willing to lose someone to win over all. The point of the game is get the king. Not the officers or the troops. Ya kill the king, you win."

"I'll keep that in mind."

"Aye, keep it in mind lad. Chess is somewhat of an obsession of mine, I think of moves all the time. If I could I would be a full time chess player, but I find myself a smuggler out of a series of misfortunate events. I'm a smuggler by virtue serendipity. There's something about you, knowing who your enemy is will save you some day. Philosophically speaking, chess is an interesting game. Even the very words check mate means the king is dead. The king is the most valuable player and must be protected at all costs, in the rear are the officers, and out front are the common soldiers, but here's the rub, at the end of the game, they all go in the same box."

The rest of the day was uneventful, but the excitement of being at sea for the first time kept Thomas feeling alive. He watched the waves from the deck and he could still see the shore. Aurella cozied up next to him as they watched the sunset. They held hands in silence.

"I wish it could be like this forever."

"What's that?" Said Aurella.

"Being at peace, in love, and feeling alive."

"What we'll do when we get to Trilliane?" She asked.

"I'll build you a house, made of stone like the one my father built. I'll start a business and we'll live happily ever after."

"Build me house will you. Do you intend to marry me?"

"Aye lassie, I do intend. We'll have two children, a boy and a girl."

"Aye lassie? One day at sea and you're talking like a sailor. Shouldn't you ask first?"

"I will when I get a ring."

"We've only known each other for two weeks. Are you so sure of your intent? I mean I had to wrangle an 'I love you' out of you as it is."

"I'm sure, never been so sure in my life."

"I'll be waiting for a ring then."

"I hope we have smooth sailing."

"I like the idea of smooth sailing. I get terrified of storms."

"Red sky at night, sailors delight. Red sky at morning, sailor take warning."

"What's that mean?"

"Something a sailor told me. It means if the sky is red we'll have good weather. If it's red in the morning, we'll get a storm."

"It's neither right now."

"I'll keep you safe either way."

She hugged him and they continued to watch the water.

The next morning, they were awakened early by the sounds of men at work loading up boats. Thomas sleepily climbed up to the deck to see what was going on. The sailors were loading up two boats full of rum. Captain Dmitry came up to Thomas.

"You can stay aboard for this one matey. Too risky, I don't want paying customers arrested for rum running their first time sailing." He gave out a boisterous laugh. "We'll set sail soon as this over, we don't dally in Storm Gap. Something's wrong about this place. It's got an evil smell to it."

"I don't even like running rum here Captain." Said the Captain's first mate. "Gives me the heebie jeebies. People there just go missing, no account'n for 'em. Never to be heard of or seen again."

"This city belongs to the Devil, that's for sure. Who in their right mind would outlaw rum in the first place?"

"Only Satan himself. That's for sure." A sailor chimed in. "I heard tale of a demon that walks that streets at night. Devouring the souls of men and then…. eating them."

"Aye it's a bad place, but there's money to be made, back to work." Captain Dmitry ordered.

Aurella was still asleep and Thomas stood on the deck, by the pale moonlight he could watch the men as they unloaded the rum on shore. A large man walked up to the Captain, shook his hand and handed him a sack of gold. They came back just as the sun started to rise.

"Shove off men, no time to waste. We can't dally here ya never know when Federation troops or boats are going to show and lock us up in the stockades. Daylights a burnin."

Thomas watched the sunrise, red sky at morning…sailor take warning.

"A storm is coming fer sure, Captain." Said the first mate.

"Aye, I see that. We have no choice, full sail, we'll try and beat the storm but we can't sit it out here. A night in Storm Gap would give me the shudders anyway."

They sailed through the day without any problems but as the afternoon wore on, the storm clouds brewed. Large black clouds and lighting took over the sky like an invading army. Thunder rolled and the waves began to get bigger and bigger, crashing over the sides. The afternoon became as black as night.

"It's going to be a big one Captain." Said the first made.

"Aye, I see that. Pull the sails down, we need to hope for the best. Everyone down below, batten the hatches."

"Everyone down below!" Captain Dmitry yelled.

Thomas and Aurella didn't hesitate, they made it for the doors leading to the lower deck. Aurella hugged Thomas once they were down below, and the ship began to rock with force.

"Keep me safe." She said.

"Where's Moshki?" Asked Thomas.

"He's still in the crow's nest." Said one of the sailors desperately.

Thomas didn't hesitate, he rushed back up the stairs and to the top deck. Aurella followed him up but stayed at the door. Thomas struggled to keep his footing on the slippery deck, a wave crashed over the side. Thomas looked up, and there was Moshki soaking wet and frightened.

"Jump Moshki! I'll catch you."

Another wave came crashing over, and Moshki gave Thomas a frightened look.

"Jump!"

Moshki closed his eyes and dropped down from the crow's nest. Thomas caught him and Aurella breathed a sigh of relief. Thomas began the precarious walk back with Moshki in his arms, stumbling trying to keep his footing as the ship rocked from the waves. Another wave came crashing over the side knocking Thomas and Moshki down to the deck. With all of his strength, Thomas slid Moshki to the door where Aurella caught him. Thomas smiled at Aurella. Another wave came crashing over, and Thomas was gone.

Aurella cried out for him, and started to go out on top but two sailors grabbed her and shut the hatch.

"No saving him lass, it's up to Davey Jones to keep him now."

Chapter 10

Ogre

Come ye'all and hear the ogre's tale, I come at night to give you fright, And to make your widows wail, I'll grind your bones between my teeth, Your marrow I find to be so sweet, Don't look behind there's no escape, I'll laugh at you, you lesser ape.

Aurella lay curled up on the floor, she hadn't slept at all and her face was red from crying. However, she knew in heart that Thomas was still alive. The storm had finally stopped in the early morning and the crew was busy cleaning up the deck. Moshki had left her be, wanting her to get some sleep. He felt guilty for Thomas being washed overboard. She pulled herself together and marched to the captain's quarters. She didn't knock, she didn't care.

"We have to go back!"

"Go back where, lass?"

"Go back from where we came from, we have to find Thomas." She started crying again.

"Oh, young lady. I'm sorry. You're going to have to accept that the sea took your man." Captain Dmitry said. "The sea has taken a lot of young men."

"He's alive. I know he's alive."

"And how do you know he's alive?"

"Because I feel it in my heart."

"Well then let's scour the sea and risk the lives of my crew members, because you have a feeling." The captain snapped at her, which he regretted the moment the words left his lips. He sighed, "Look lass, even if he is still alive, we could spend months looking for him, it's a big sea. A lot of salty, briny water and he's six hours behind us. I wouldn't even know where to start looking for him."

"We have to try."

"No lass, I can't. If he's still alive he'll make it to shore."

"Can you take me back then? I'll look for him on my own."

"I can't do that either, were too far gone. It's a one-month journey to Trilliane, when we get there I will give you free passage back."

Six hours earlier it was still dark, the waves were ten feet high and a torrential rain beat down. A half full barrel of rum bobbed up and down with the waves nonchalantly, oblivious that there was a storm raging about the sea. A rope dangled from the barrel, floated alongside in a twisted mess. The barrel had been swept off the Pale Witch along with Thomas, yet the barrel wasn't as sorely missed. Lightning lit the sky, and flashed with regularity. A hand broke the surface of the water and grabbed hold of the rope. It was Thomas. He had seen the barrel but no sign of the Pale Witch. He swallowed a lot of water, coughing and spitting he pulled himself to the barrel. He tried to get on top of the barrel, but as barrels usually do in water when top heavy, he spun and dunked Thomas one more time. He held on to the rope, and just tried to keep his head above sea level. A daunting task. He floated on the barrel until the morning, the storm ceased and he washed up onto a beach. And that's where he laid, passed out and tired. He didn't move.

Unkh Headknocker was ten feet tall, broad shouldered and bald. He wore loose fitting pants and very large sandals. The muscles on his shoulders bulged, he had no neck to speak of. He preferred loose fitting clothing including his shirts because his legs were like tree trunks and his arms were strong enough to carry a horse. His large nose added no beauty to his face and you could paint a mural on his forehead. He was an ogre. He was old, over fifty was old for an ogre and on cold nights his bones ached and his muscles twitched.

Unkh Headknocker was an ogre of ill repute, he was an outcast from his clan because he had lost the taste of war. He contemplated this as he walked along the beach. He had lost his taste for battle, and wanted only to be philosopher instead. The ogres are a warrior class and are willing to do battle with anyone, goblins, dargons, but especially humans. When he told his elders his intentions he was told there was no need for philosophers, to die in battle was the ultimate death of a warrior. After much deliberation, instead of killing him they decided to banish him. He had lived a life in peace along the ocean beach ever since, but it was a lonely existence. He built a house barely perceptible to the human eye from rocks, logs and stone. He lived off the land, fished and stole a few sheep here and there. He liked to learn about healing and medicine, studying some old books written humans. He spent much of his time reading and collecting things, he liked to collect pieces of glass washed up along the shore and he spent many hours skipping rocks.

He was busy collecting glass and skipping flat rocks along the water's surface. He found a very perfect rounded and flat rock, placed it between his thumb and forefinger and sent it sailing.

"52." He said to himself. "New rock skipping record. Maybe of all time." Being all alone, Unkh had taken to talking to himself. It didn't bother him, he just worried about the day he would start an argument.

Unkh noticed the barrel from a distance, a perpetual scrounger never passes on an opportunity, and a barrel was an opportunity. Lots of things washed up to shore, humans were always losing things at sea. A barrel was a good find, it could have ham, dried fish, bread, or even his favorite, rum. Ogres liked their drink, rum was fine but whiskey is better Unkh always thought. He hoped for whiskey.

He neared the barrel and saw the writing on the side.

"Rum, it will do. But there's one of those things attached to it."

Unkh looked over the thing snarled up in a rope and lying face down in the sand.

"A human."

Unkh placed the palm of his massive hand on the human's back and gave a push. Thomas gushed out a pint of sea water, then coughed and sputtered.

"Still alive. Hmmm interesting."

Unkh picked Thomas up by his shirt and carried him like a grocery bag, he then heaved the barrel of rum over one shoulder and headed back to his home. His morning fire was still burning and a blackened pot was steaming his lunch slowly. He dropped Thomas near the fire without any gentleness at all, grabbed a tremendous sized mug and cracked open the barrel.

He shook his head in disappointment. "Half empty." He took a gulp and sat down, stirring his lunch with large wooden spoon. It was getting chillier, must be late September now, he thought. He would have to trade in his sandals for his boots.

Thomas couldn't move. He could barely open an eye, his left eye seemed to be swollen shut. His body ached, his head hurt and stomach was queasy. But he was surprised to find himself alive, or at least he thought he was alive. Being dead probably wouldn't hurt as much. He coughed up some salt water and opened his right eye wider seeing the ogre sitting on a log nonchalantly drinking rum from a mug. He saw the fire with the large black kettle boiling something, and he did not want to know what was inside. He still couldn't move and he wondered if he was tied up. Surely he was, the ogre most definitely intended to cook him, eat him and even make a casserole for later. He was numb, and he tried to speak.

"I Ooofla sufga." Was what he managed to say, and he even realized it was gibberish.

"That's a strange language, human. I've been around awhile and I have never heard that tongue spoken before."

Thomas mustered his strength, and lifted his head a little. "I survived the sea, only to be eaten by an ogre." He managed to utter.

Unkh laughed. "I've no intentions of eating you, but a kind thanks for the rum."

"Why do you have me tied up?"

"You're not tied up, little man. You just can't move."

"You've drugged me?"

"No. You're free, you're probably just still cold and numb. Sit by the fire and warm yourself. Dry off. You're free to go but I'll be keeping the rum. Payment of sorts."

"Payment?"

"Why yes, I saved your life, pushed a good pint or two of sea water out of your lungs, and likely you would have died of a chill. You're welcome."

"Thank you."

Thomas let his head rest down again. "Why are you saving me? Ogres are evil man-eating beasts."

"In my old age, I've grown wiser. And believe it or not humans are not that tasty."

"I think I'll just lie here for a bit."

"Wise decision."

Thomas fell back asleep.

Thomas stood on a field, there was a tower nearby and a dargon popped its head out of a doorway at the top of the tower, it sneered at Thomas and growled as it began to descend the stairs. Another when came out and another. Thomas was scared, terrified. His heart raced and He was alone. He pulled his out his bow and reached for an arrow, but his quiver was empty. The dargons slowly descended the stairs and then began to circle him. He reached for his, sword, it wasn't there, he reached for his knife and it was gone. He remembered how he lost his sword on the field of battle and was crushed by a dead dargon. He was unarmed. A dargon leapt at him, knocking him down. Another lunged for his throat.

He awoke still next the fire, it was dusk and the ogre was either gone or inside his home. A lone cricket chirped to an even beat. It was just a nightmare and Thomas was sweating and breathing hard. The numbness was gone and he could move. He got up and looked around, he couldn't leave even if he wanted to, there seemed no way out of the ogres little camp. His house looked normal aside from the fact that the door was twelve feet tall and the house itself was about fourteen feet high.

Bazaal perched in a tree nearby, snickering. He found the human boy by accident when leaving Storm Gap. Seen the little wretch of all things on a ship. He crept aboard while it was dusk and hid behind a load of supplies. He climbed to the top of a mast during the storm and watched with delight when Thomas was washed overboard. It wasn't easy following him to shore in the waves and the storm but he managed. His master would be pleased again.

Thomas was hungry and he dared to knock on the door. Imagine knocking on an ogre's door and asking for help. He was hungry, famished. This ogre was perplexing Thomas, everything he was over told said they were violent and bloodthirsty. Unkh opened the door and glowered down on Thomas.

Thomas nervously held his ground. "Why didn't you kill me?"

"I've lost my will to kill, human." He said. "And you? You knocked on my door, a human that shows manners to an ogre. Very strange."

"I'm sorry to bother you, I'm very hungry and still tired. I don't know how to get out of here and don't know which way to go."

Unkh hesitated, looked the boy up and down and snorted.

Thomas still held his ground, if the ogre was going to kill him he would have done it by now. "My name is Thomas, Thomas Kray." He trembled as the ogre bared his top fangs that could easily be mistaken for small tusks.

"Unkh Headknocker. Come in. I would shake your hand but I think that I would crush your puny little hand."

"Yes, let's do away with that formality." Said Thomas.

"There's food on the table. I just ate."

Thomas eyed the food on the table, he recognized bread, butter and some apples. The pot on the fire contained a gooey brown mess.

Unkh noticed Thomas eyeing the pot. "Lamb stew, human. It has potatoes, carrots and herbs. Eat it before I change my mind about my hospitality."

There were two massive chairs and Thomas climbed up one and sat down. Thomas was tall, over six feet, but he felt like a two-year-old sitting at his mother's table. He had a nice view of the rim of the plate. If Unkh could have shaken his head, he would of but he had no neck. He grabbed a few books from a shelf and placed them on the chair for Thomas to sit on. Thomas felt even more like a child but he placed his pride aside and ate.

Thomas looked around at Unkh's house, small for an ogre but huge for a human. There were books everywhere. On shelves, on end tables, on the kitchen table, and over the mantle on the fire. There were books stuffed in odd places, such in the bread basket. Above the books on the mantle was a tomahawk by ogre standards, an axe too large to wield by human ones. By the tomahawk was a mace dangling from a chain as big as man's head. A pipe the size of a chimney laid on at the kitchen table next to a candle as big as Thomas's arm.

"This is good, thank you." Said Thomas. "I apologize for my rudeness."

"It's ok, I understand. It's not like my brethren haven't earned that reputation. As for myself, I've never cared for the taste of human, too gamey."

That statement did nothing to ease Thomas's tension. He was glad this ogre was not a hungry one, because with enough spices Thomas could become a decent meal.

"You have a lot of books." Thomas said.

"Good friends, good books and a sleepy conscience: this is the ideal life. A human said that."

"Where did you get all of them?"

"Some are ogre books I've collected, some human. Once a trunk washed up ashore full of books and luckily none were waterlogged. The human ones are hard to read; I need a magnifying glass for the small print. Do you read?"

"No, I don't know how."

"Very pitiful. Everyone should read."

"I had a book, given to me by my father but I think I lost it in the storm."

"What was it?"

"I don't know, I held on to it hoping someone would explain it to me. But I don't read."

"I see. A loss of a book is like losing a friend."

"I lost a friend… in battle. It was nothing like losing a book."

"Well said. Where are you going?"

"I was sailing to Trilliane."

"Never heard of it."

"It's an island, free of war and the stench of the dargon. I've lost my father, my mother, friends and comrades. The girl I love is heading there, along with a good friend, I hope they make it safe."

"Love, interesting concept."

"Ogres don't love?" Thomas asked.

"Ogre women are a brutish lot. I never saw the need for one."

"Well I'm in love. I will do everything to get to her. I'm in love with her and she is so much better than me. I will do everything to find her."

"I see. Winter is coming, soon. There won't be any more of your sailing ships this time of year."

Thomas sunk his head into his hands in resignation. "I've nowhere to go, I've no money. Nothing. Everything I had was on the ship."

Unkh looked at the boy. Thought for a moment. He thought some more. Thomas became a little nervous at the look on his face.

"You're in a dilemma indeed." He finally said and then he stroked his chin. Ogres cannot grow beards but if he had one he would be stroking his beard in a ponderous way like an old scholar. A philosopher.

"Winter is coming." Unkh said.

"Yes I know, you just said that."

"You should stay here for now. A puny human would never withstand the winter. You have no clothes… no prospects. You're a mess."

"Thank you for pointing that out, I hadn't realized my situation till you pointed it out."

"Sarcasm. I like it. I have an extra room. There's no bed but there is a soft carpet and I have some furs. There's a fireplace in there and more books."

"Why would you help me?"

"Redemption. Besides you're pathetic."

"Thank you."

"You'll be doing me a favor. I've grown pretty lonely these years. Even human company is better than nothing."

"You said redemption. What do you mean?"

Unkh gave a grunt and then he thought some more. "I've killed a lot of men, in battle and for sport. I did it because it was our way. To be a good ogre you had to be battle hardened. Strong. We even war among ourselves. Down in my soul, I knew it was wrong, to kill for no reason. To kill for defense is another but for no reason… I just couldn't do it anymore."

"So you helping me will help you?"

"I hope so. My clan cast me out ten years past. I've been living alone here, just on the border of human and ogre eyes. This is no man's land… and no ogre's land."

"Well thank you again for your hospitality."

"Well you will earn your keep, and I will teach you to read."

"I think I would like that."

"Can you hunt?"

"I'm the best there is. What do you like?"

"Sheep, they don't take much hunting skill but I love a roast mutton." Unkh laughed.

"I can get us some venison."

"I like venison. I guess it's settled, you can stay here a while, when you are fully recovered fully I will guide you to the human city, Storm Gap. I have devoted these last ten years studying books, medicine, history, and philosophy. I've never had anyone to heal. Let me see your wounds there, little Thomas."

Thomas showed him the bruises from the battle, his ribcage was black and there was a rope burn."

"I'll make a poultice; it will draw the bruise out. That's serious bruising. How did you get it?"

"A dargon collapsed on me when I killed it."

"A scourge upon the land for ogres and men alike. They do nothing but destroy, even the land."

"Have you fought them too?"

"Yes. Ogres are big but few in number. Those things can swarm an ogre."

"Why are there so few of you?"

"Again, ogre women are a terrible lot."

"That's saying a lot for an ogre."

Unkh sneered at Thomas, but then laughed. "Aye, I guess it does. Here wrap this around your chest." Unkh handed him a linen soaked in herbs and warm water. "Get some rest human. Tomorrow is a new day."

Thomas had no trouble falling asleep again. Bazaal was outside the window, staring in. Waiting for his moment. It was coming soon. He loved to send out nightmares. He drifted off to a nearby branch and began to think. Bazaal was devious but originality was not a strong suit.

"Maybe the same nightmare as this morning." Bazaal said. He rubbed his hands together. "Reoccurring nightmares are fun."

Unkh woke up from a peaceful slumber. Something was wrong, he could sense it. He got up and pulled his pants on. It was the middle of the night, the time when demons were about. Unkh smelled a demon. Unkh looked at the human, who had fallen asleep on his kitchen floor in front of the fire. Thomas was tossing and turning, the poultice he made had wrought itself free from his body. He smelled the demon even stronger now, it was because the demon was working. When they worked the smell was unbearable. He grabbed the mace from above the mantle. Unkh changed his mind, laid the mace on the table and picked up the tomahawk.

Unkh stepped outside, the smell of demon was stronger even though there was a cold breeze blowing. Unkh looked up in the tree and there was the demon, black and fat sitting on a tree limb. The demon was in some sort of trance and didn't even notice Unkh step outside. Unkh nimbly flipped the tomahawk in his hand and threw. Bazaal was split in two, and black blood gushed down the tree. The tomahawk planted itself squarely into tree where it stopped with brain matter stuck to the haft.

Unkh slapped his hands together and reached up to retrieve his weapon. The tree smoldered from the dripping acidic blood.

"Now I can get some sleep." He said.

Thomas woke up, the nightmare from the night drifted from his memory and instead he thought of Aurella. He thought of her beauty, the way she made him laugh, her smile and her wonderment. He couldn't stop being in love with her though she was miles away. He was haunted by her last kiss, and the way they made love. We will be together again he thought to himself. No matter what it would take to get to her. He would climb mountains and sail the ocean for her.

Unkh was at the kitchen table when Thomas awoke. He was on his third cup of coffee and smoking his pipe. He looked at the stirring human with wonder, the demon had been sent for him. Why would this scrawny boy be of such importance? Sending a demon is no easy feat. A necromancer was after him.

"You had a visitor last night." He said tugging at his pipe.

"A visitor?"

"Aye, a demon one. Nasty little thing. What's a demon going after you for?"

"I didn't know one was after me."

"Have you been plagued by nightmares?"

"Yes, how did you know?"

"Black little demon was perched on my tree last night. Bazaal is its name. Nasty thing. He's the demon of nightmares."

Thomas suddenly remembered the beast on the plain of battle. "Nightmares in and nightmares out. It's just business."

"What's that you say?"

"A few days ago, when I was crushed by the dargon. A fat little flying thing said that to me, I just now remembered."

"Aye, that's the one. He won't be bothering anytime soon."

"What happened?"

"I split him in two pieces like a grapefruit."

"You killed him?"

"No, you can't kill a demon. But I sent him back to where he came from, the depths of hell. You must be someone important, that demon was after you."

Thomas looked out the window at the scarred tree. "Why would a demon be after me?"

"You tell me. He was after you." Unkh grabbed a couple a dozen eggs. "Do you want some breakfast?"

"I'm starved."

"How many eggs do you want?"

"Two is fine."

Unkh shrugged and grabbed two more eggs. "You eat so little, I won't have to worry about feeding you."

"If you want me to hunt, I should worry about feeding you!"

"You're funny human. How do you feel about learning to read?"

"You're going to teach me to read?"

"I told you I would. Aye, we start with the abc's."

"I just find it strange an ogre would take the time to teach a human to read."

"I've nothing better to do, and neither do you."

The time went by very quickly and winter set in. A thick snow covered the ogre's grotto in mid-December. Hunting was easier because Thomas could track deer and antelope. Unkh still went out and brought home a cow or a sheep. A fire always burned in Unkh's home and survival was the daily work schedule. Thomas was learning to read simple children's books and it seemed to Thomas that Unkh really enjoyed teaching him. Unkh gave him lessons every evening after hunting and Thomas realized that he enjoyed learning. Thomas's father read but he never had the time to teach him. Unkh was amazed at how fast Thomas was actually learning, in a few short weeks Thomas progressed from abc's to full sentences.

"You're ready for more mature books now I think." Unkh said. "Here's a poem written by a human a very long time ago. Read it aloud for me would you."

Thomas began reading, "A dream. In visions of the dark night, I have dreamed of joy departed- But a waking dream of life and light, hath left me broken hearted."

"Very good, keep going." Said Unkh.

"Ah! What is not a dream by day, to him whose eyes are cast, on things around him with a ray, turned back upon the past? That holy dream- that holy dream, while all the world were chiding, hath cheered me as a lovely beam, a lonely spirit guiding. What though that light, thro' storm and night, so trembled from afar- what could there be more purely bright, in truth's day-star."

Thomas paused as he finished the poem. "It's as if that poem was written about me."

"A good poem is written to reach the heart of everyone."

"I have to find Aurella. She's all I ever think about. In the evening when I try to sleep I think of her. I wake up thinking of her. I love her so much and it hurts to be away from her."

"Spring will soon be here. I would bet she may come looking for you as well."

"I don't know if I can wait till spring."

"Spring comes early here, we are much farther south than where you are from, Trilliane is even warmer but boats don't sail because of the storms. The soonest you could sail there is in a month. I'll take you to Storm Gap then."

Aurella and Moshki walked off the ship, the Pale Witch would be docked there for a week. She carried the leather satchel that belonged to Thomas, clutching on to it for dear life. She had stuffed the book inside of it is well, Thomas had dropped as he saved Moshki and it bounced down the stairs.

"Moshki, do you have any money?"

"A melfling always has money"

"Can I borrow some?"

"You have an entire sack full in your hands."

"This is Thomas's money; I dare not spend it."

"I don't think he would mind if we spent a little."

"I won't, he trusts me. I cannot!"

"Fine, lunch is on me."

"It's truly beautiful here, I wish he was here with us."

"Everything will be alright, we'll find him."

"You'll go back with me?"

"Of course, I've nothing better to do, besides I owe him my life. According to melfling code, I must repay him. The melfling code is a serious matter."

"Thank you, Moshki." Aurella bent down and gave him a big hug and kissed him on the cheek. Moshki blushed but you couldn't see it through his furry face.

"We have a long time here, let's make the best of it." Moshki said, "We'll find an inn, I'm tired of sleeping on ships."

"Me too. Real food would be splendid."

The months went by quickly and Captain Dmitry was surprised when they showed up to set sail back to the Four Corners.

"What's yer destination, lass. I'm a man of my word, I promised I would take you back free of charge and I will hold to that."

"Storm Gap. I figure that's the most likely place he would go."

"You're chasing a ghost lass. But I wish the best of luck to you. Another month we'll be there."

"Hello Captain." Moshki said with relish.

"Moshki, welcome aboard sir mouse. Good to have you aboard again."

"And thank you good Captain."

"I'll take you two to Storm Gap. But be warned it is an evil place. Death roams the streets. A sinister cloud hangs over it. The people are strange. Wizards and witches rule the city. Keep your wits about you."

Chapter 11

Love lost

When shall we three meet again? In thunder, lightning, or in rain? When the hurlyburly's done, When the battle's lost and won. That will be ere the set of sun.

-Shakespeare, Macbeth

Ravana stepped out unto her balcony and looked down, it was still chilly as spring began to melt some of the snow. By the light of a street lamp she could see a poor man walking right underneath. Nothing more than a beggar. Probably homeless. She mustered up a wad and let her spit go straight down on top his head. She giggled and stepped back from the light of her room. The man felt his hair and looked up at the sky as if it was raining. She giggled some more.

She walked back into her room where two other girls her age were dancing in the moonlight. Not really her friends, but more like co-workers, they were her sisters of the coven. On the floor in black charcoal they had drawn a circle, in the circle a five pointed star, in the star at all five points were runes of an ancient nature.

"It's so wonderful your father approves of our practice." Said one, her name was Samara. She was a chunky little girl with blonde hair and a freckled complexion. To look at her you would think she was a simple farm girl but she had a heart of stone so cold it would freeze your soul.

"My father would never approve either, witchcraft is the devil's work he says." Said Regan, the third of their little trio. Regan was pale with red hair, so skinny she looked as if she would break in half if the wind blew to hard.

"It is the devil's work fool." Said Ravana.

"Yes I know, but I go to church on Sundays with my father."

"So stop going."

"Never, I want to inherit my father's money."

Samara giggled, "You won't have to wait long as old as your father is."

"Shut up, at least I have a father."

"Your father's so old he looks like death warmed over."

Regan picked up a sacrificial knife and held it up over her head as if to stab Samara. Samara shrieked and cowered on the floor.

"Girls!" Ravana grabbed the knife from Regan. "We have business at hand."

"I don't know why you are so touchy; you want your father dead anyhow." Samara pouted.

"What have you planned for us Ravana?" Regan sneered at Samara as she asked.

Samara snapped out of her pouting as if nothing had happened. "Yes do tell. Conjuring? Incantations?"

"How about a curse!" Shouted Regan forgetting just as easily.

"Oooh, a curse." Hissed Samara.

The two of them joined hands and danced around the circle, Ravana lit a black candle and placed it in the center of the drawn circle on the floor.

"A curse it is. A curse it shall be. And who shall we curse?"

"I know, my father." Regan chimed. "I won't have to go to church on Sunday!"

"So shall it be." Said Ravana.

"So shall it be!" The other two chorused.

Thomas was packing a backpack he had made weeks ago from deer hide. Today was the day he would set forth in search of Aurella. Thomas could easily just walk along the shoreline to get to Storm Gap, but Unkh had grown fond of Thomas and wanted to see that he made it safely there. They would take a back trail there through the woods.

They set out without talking and walked through the day. The hidden grotto that Unkh lived in was left behind, the passage inside was well hidden by trees and bushes. Thomas wondered how he found it in the first place. Unkh was sullen and somber. He carried a large walking stick, at least three feet taller than Thomas. Thomas realized he had never walked with Unkh during their time together, and he found it difficult to keep up with his pace. Thomas was used to walking slowly, and stealthily. Unkh walked with huge strides and Thomas realized he needed to jog just to keep up.

Unkh was sullen because he was losing a friend. A good friend. It occurred to him he had never had a friend before. An odd thing friendship. It can be found and lost with but a blink of an eye. He really hoped that Thomas would find his true love. As an ogre he had given up on true love, but understood the concept from reading his books. He wondered if there was an ogre girl out there somewhere for him, someone with the soul of a poet and the passion for love.

They reached the edge of the forest at dawn.

"There lies Storm Gap, human."

The city was visible a long way off but the lights could be seen as the sun set on the horizon.

"Unkh, we've known each other awhile, you can call me Thomas."

"This is as far as I can take you… Thomas. I would be risking my own life if I took you any further."

"You shouldn't have taken me at all, but I appreciate it."

Thomas grabbed Unkh's forearm and Unkh his.

"I'll see you again Unkh, I have a feeling our paths will cross again."

Unkh leaned forward on his walking stick. "Find your love Thomas. Find your love."

It dawned on Thomas that his troubles could only be beginning. He had no money, no job skills and certainly no one he could call on for help. Still this was the first step forward to finding Aurella. He crossed the large field between the forest and Storm Gap with the sloppiness that a spring thaw brings. Mud and muck at every step. Patches of snow were everywhere but he would make it.

Walking in through the gates of the city, there was a large tent. It was the only tent in the city, amongst many solid stone structures of regular buildings. It was a simple tent sewn to together from many colorful patches of blankets. The tent held a large banner, and Thomas was delighted to be able to read the sign. Uncle Billy's Revival.

"Holy, holy." A man dressed in black shouted to him as he tried to walked by, the man blocked Thomas's way. Thomas was taken aback at his abrupt nature.

"Excuse me." Thomas said, trying to go around.

"Have you been saved boy?"

"I don't think so." Thomas said. "Now if you would just let me go around…"

The man cut him short. "There is no around boy. You need to repent of your sins."

Thomas looked blankly at the man, wondering what his intentions were. However, he suddenly realized that he had been saved, Unkh most certainly had saved him, but for some reason Thomas knew it wasn't what the strange little fellow meant. He was odd, with a hooked nose and a bowl haircut. His hair was jet black and his face was gaunt, he was skinny as rail post but at least a full foot shorter than Thomas. Thomas didn't like him from the start. From inside the tent, a chorus of women began to sing a gospel tune. He tried to push past him, but the man stopped him, placing his hand on his chest.

"Foul abominations walk the earth boy. The end is at hand and death draws near."

"I've seen death; he looks a little like you." Thomas said. "What are you talking about, abominations?"

The man was unfazed by the comment. "Ogres and melflings."

"Ogres and melflings are what they are, they've done no harm to me." Thomas tried again to push passed him but was stopped once more.

"Heed my words boy. Those that turn their eye to the work of the evil one is no different from the evil one. Repent now and take up the sword against the abominations."

"You're asking me to kill a melfling?" Thomas was quickly tiring of this man calling him boy all the time.

"Aye lad. They're a blight, a curse upon the land. All creatures not of the original creations are abominations. It's not natural, it's not normal my son. We must do what we can to eradicate them. God hates melflings."

Thomas began to wonder if this was how the war between men and ogres began, because of some petty man worrying about what was natural. "I'm not your son. I think you worship the god of your imaginations, you just call him by the same name."

"You're are a wicked one. There is no rest for the wicked."

"Well you are correct on that one, I get no rest, no sleep. But I still won't follow you."

"Oh now, I feel the spirit coming upon me." He said as he began to shake in convulsions and he fell to the ground. A crowd of people gathered around and Thomas seized the moment to walk away from him. He wanted to get as far away from him as possible.

He walked into the center of the city, there was a park and he sat down on a bench. He was tired and had nowhere to go, and it was now dark. Thomas thought of Aurella, and he remembered the words that came to him months ago when they were still at her father's house. He now was able to read and write thanks to Unkh and he pulled out a pen and a notebook and wrote the words down.

For Aurella:

> Thinking of you keeps me awake.
> Dreaming of you keeps me asleep.
> Being with you keeps me alive.

He could see her face and he reached out to touch her but his hand just touched the air. He stuck the notebook back in his pocket. The bench seemed as good a place as any and he laid down and fell asleep.

From her balcony Ravana looked down on Thomas and she was taken aback. He was surely handsome; like no other boy she had seen before. Samara and Regan stepped out on the balcony as well.

"Ooh, candy." Said Regan, checking out Thomas as well.

"Eyes off him, I claim him."

"And how is that?" Asked Regan. "He looks like fair game."

"I saw him first." Said Ravana.

"Seems like a game is at play." Samara said. "I'm just wondering why he was reaching out like that, seems kind of odd."

"Regan, do you think a skinny bitch like you stands a chance with him? You're fooling yourself." Replied Ravana.

"We'll see."

"I think we should let him choose, I stand a chance as well." Said Samara.

The other two looked at her and laughed with derision.

"You're the exact opposite of Regan, you're a chubby little thing, why you would certainly smother him on the night of your consummation."

"Wench, you are incredibly cruel." Samara shot back. "He would have nothing to do with you after he gets to know you. Your personality overshadows your looks. That's why no man has ever stayed with you."

"I will remedy that. "Perhaps you two hags would like to make a wager." Ravana said.

"Betting on who gets his gets him first?" Regan asked.

"Certainly."

"You're on, but what shall we bet?" Asked Regan.

"I get both your wands."

"Fine, I get your spell book." Said Regan.

"And I get your wand." Said Samara.

"Deal, now get out, I grow tired of your company."

"Kicking us out are you?" They said at the same time.

"Yes, be gone pests."

The two of them stormed out of the bedroom and down the stairs together. "She's up to something." Said Ravana.

"No doubt about it." Samara said matter of fact.

Ravana went back to the circle, removed the black candle and replaced it with a pink one. She opened her spell book and flipped the pages to a love spell. She read through the ingredients required, and realized she needed a personal item from the boy on the bench. Funny she thought, I don't even know his name yet.

"I shall own him. A delightful play thing."

The Prince walked into his daughter's room, the door was left open. Ravana was delving into her spell book.

"What is it father?" She snapped.

"Nothing, just came in to see how you and your friends were coming along."

"We've made a bet."

"Really. And what is this one about? Who can summon the biggest monster?"

"No this one is about a boy."

"A boy?"

"Yes," She sighed. "The one who gets the boy on the bench on the street down there."

The Prince walked to the balcony to see what she was all in a flutter about.

"Look at him. He seems like a muddy street urchin to me."

The Prince suddenly cocked his head to look at the boy closer, and he realized with amazement that it was Thomas Kray. The very boy he had been searching for months, sending out that incompetent demon Bazaal who never returned. Reforming another group of men for a search party that turned up no results. Sending spies and assassins throughout the Four Corners and across the seas to no avail, and now the boy shows up at his very doorstep. But what of the key? The book that held everything in the balance of his power. Was it still in his possession? He had to find out before disposing of him.

Ravana stepped alongside him, "I want him father."

"I...want to talk to him." He said. "Come, we can't have him sleeping outside."

They walked outside to where he lay on the bench. Ravana slid next to him and stroked his hair. Thomas awoke with a start, blinking from a hard slumber and wondering who the strange man staring down at him was. He felt the touch of Ravana and jerked away, shaking his head.

"Whaa...?" Was all he could utter in his surprise.

"What's your name young man?" Asked The Prince.

Thomas was still stunned. "Thomas." He managed.

"What are you doing out on this bench? Loitering and sleeping on the bench is illegal in my city."

"Leave him alone father."

Thomas looked upon Ravana, she looked like a crouching cat ready to pounce.

"I'm sorry I had nowhere to go. I was swept off a ship months ago and was stranded. I managed to survive the winter through the help of a stranger." Thomas omitted the small tidbit that said stranger was an ogre. "I made way here after the thaw, it was the closest city."

"Well we can't have you staying out here. You will catch a death chill."

"Come inside, I will take care of you." Said Ravana.

For Thomas, those words from her were not comforting. Something about her sent off a prickly feeling in his skin. Thomas staggered into their house, a small castle rather, he was still feeling sleepy and his legs were like rubber from trotting through the mud field to Storm Gap. They brought him in and set him down next to a roaring fire.

"Drink this." The Prince offered.

"What is it?"

"Brandy, very old. It will warm you."

Thomas took a sip and he felt better. He took another and felt warm all over.

"Slow down. Too much will have the opposite effect."

"You said you were in a shipwreck?" Asked Ravana, leaning into him very closely.

"No, I was on a ship set for Trilliane. We ran into a storm and I was washed over by a wave trying to help a friend."

"Is he ok now?" Asked Ravana, feigning interest.

"I think so. He made it to the cabin area."

"Why were you sailing to Trilliane?"

Thomas hesitated being weary of not revealing too much about his fighting in the war and deserting. "To start a new life with a girl. We were going to marry. I wanted to start a life free from the worries of the dargon horde."

Ravana frowned at hearing of this girl.

"There's a war going on, we can't have everyone just leaving this land. If everyone left, there would be no defense."

Thomas stumbled, realizing he had already said too much to the wrong person. "I realize that sir, but I felt I was too young at the time."

"Ridiculous. You're the perfect age." The Prince chided him. He eyed him up and down and wondered if the book was in his possession. "What's your surname?" He asked, knowing full well what it was but The Prince did not lay all his knowledge out like some fool, he knew how to play his cards.

"Kray, I'm Thomas Kray."

"Thomas Kray? Son of Lord Holden Kray of Greystone?"

"Yes sir, that's me."

"I knew your father; he was killed at the battle of the Citadel. I would not expect the son of Lord Kray to run away like a scared rabbit."

"I'm sorry sir, I didn't know what to do at the time and I was tasked by the father of the girl I love to protect her. I just wanted to get her to safety."

"Leave him alone father." Scolded Ravana.

The Prince ignored her, "I see, a noble enough cause I suppose."

"Ravana, can I see you in private a moment."

They walked out of the room but Thomas still felt tense. There was something wrong and the man was making him feel ill at ease. He realized they hadn't told him their names as yet, which was even more maddening.

"Father please leave him alone, I told you will I'm going to have him. He's mine."

"Ravana this is the very boy I have been searching for. He is in possession of a book that could cause a revolt in this country. The very revolt I'm trying to end. It's bad enough religion is spreading everywhere. It's foothold of rebellion has even taken seed in this very city, with some very notable converts."

"Oh so that's what this is about, you losing power."

"If I lose power, you lose yours. Our castle, our way of life will be gone. People could rise up against us and destroy us. I care not for your current infatuation I care for my power, a power that will someday belong to you as well."

Ravana gave into resignation, but reasoned with her father. "There's no need to kill him, he can be my play thing and I will get this precious book for you."

"Take him upstairs and show him to the spare room. Search his clothing."

"Search his clothing? What, you want me to just start taking his clothes off?" Ravana laughed.

"Figure out a way with a little more subtlety."

"Yes father."

They went back out to Thomas.

"As a son of Lord Kray you must stay as a guest of our house, royalty, even our lower ones shouldn't be sleeping in the streets like some vagabond."

Thomas bit his tongue at the underhanded comment about his lower nobility but he didn't have much of a choice. "I don't even know your names."

"Of course, how rude of me. This is my daughter Ravana, and I'm simply called The Prince. You may refer to me as such."

"Thank you for letting me stay."

"Ravana will show you to your room."

"Come Thomas. Come upstairs and follow me."

He followed her upstairs, it was very late in the evening by now and Thomas was tired after the drink. Ravana made him feel uncomfortable still, he didn't like the way she looked at him. They got to the room, and to add to the discomfort she followed him in.

"Take off those dreadful clothes." Ravana said.

"Excuse me?"

"Your clothes are filthy; I will have our servants clean them. They will be ready for you by morning."

"Do you mind turning your head?"

"Oh, a shy boy." She turned around, but watched him undress through a mirror. A sly grin covered her face. He was just as nice without clothes she thought.

"You can just wear a blanket, shy boy."

"Here," He said. "Thanks for taking care of my clothes, I guess they were pretty dirty."

"I suppose you just have one set of clothes."

"Yes. The rest of my clothes are on a ship."

"We'll see about getting you more, I'll take you shopping tomorrow. These clothes are dreadful even if they were clean."

"You're too kind to me. Why are you helping me out?"

"Oh I have my reasons shy boy."

Ravana went straight to her father.

"There's nothing in his clothes, but he still has a backpack."

"I'll look through that tomorrow, find a way to distract him."

"I already have that covered, I'm taking him shopping tomorrow."

"You are a clever little girl."

Ravana left her father's library and took a dagger from her side, cutting a small piece of cloth from Thomas's shirt. She woke one of the servants and charged them with washing his clothes. She didn't care it was late. She went to her room with the small piece of cloth and began her spell. She lit the pink candle in the middle of the circle on the floor. She burned the piece of cloth over the candle and threw it on the floor, mixing the ashes with lavender, and then said the spell out loud.

>Dark of night, darkness divine
>Bring Thomas's heart to mine,
>On this night send him to me,
>To come in submission and harmony,
>His heart and mind belongs to me,
>From this day forth in sanctity.

Thomas woke up the next morning in a sweat, and the first time he didn't think of Aurella. He woke up confused and dazed wondering where he was. He suddenly remembered the events of last night. He remembered The Prince and his daughter Ravana. Ravana he thought. She was beautiful and he couldn't understand his aversion to her last night. She had been kind to him in every way. He loved her, no wait Aurella he thought. And the memory of her faded. Aurella who? He closed his eyes and could not recall her face. The front of his head was numb and he stumbled as he got out of bed.

"Get up shy boy."

Thomas quickly wrapped the blanket around him. Ravana was never up this early, she usually slept through the morning till noon, she hated the light and loved the darkness. But this morning she had a mission and she wanted to flaunt her new play thing in front of those two bitches, Regan and Samara.

"Here are your clothes, I had a servant wash and dry them last night." Ravana said.

Thomas looked at his shirt.

"Is there something wrong darling?" She asked.

She called him darling as if they were married and Thomas grew more confused. "Well, there's a piece torn from the corner of my shirt, I'll need to fix."

"Don't be silly, you can throw out those rags after today, we can go to the bazaar and get you new ones this morning."

"I don't have any money."

"Don't worry your pretty little head. My father is very wealthy; he already gave me the money to get some things for you."

"Ravana?"

"Yes?"

"Your name is very pretty, and thank you for all that you and father are doing for me."

Ravana smiled, the spell had worked. "Well thank you for the compliment. Now put your clothes on."

He stood there for a moment looking at her.

"Still shy I see, very well. I'll turn around."

"I would kind of prefer that you left the room."

The spell needs a little tweaking she thought. "Fine, you can have your privacy."

The bazaar was full of wonders for Thomas. Ravana picked out clothes for him, clothes that he would have never picked out.

"What do you think of this shirt?" She asked.

"It's a bit fancy for my tastes." He said looking at the frilly shirt.

"Nonsense, you can't walk around looking like a farmhand your entire life."

He tried the clothes on and she insisted he wear them leaving the bazaar. Thomas didn't put up a fight, he did what she asked. But he felt uncomfortable and felt like people were staring at him.

"Ravana." He stumbled over her name.

"Yes darling?"

"There's something I want to tell you. I know this is soon but I feel like I have to say it."

"What is it? Just say it shy boy."

"I love you."

"I know you do, darling." Ravana spotted Samara and Regan. "Come I want to show you off to my friends."

Samara and Regan were in the bazaar shopping as well; it was all they ever did. In fact, it was Ravana's only hobby as well.

"Girls, girls. How are you?" Ravana asked.

"Oh you know, just out spending father's money." Regan said, "Funny he woke up with a terrible case of boils all over his body this morning."

"Who is this young man you're with?" Samara asked.

"Oh, you don't recognize him? This is the same young man on the bench from last night."

Samara and Regan both gasped.

"Well I hardly recognize him; he was in rags last night. Handsome however." Regan said.

"Thomas blushed.

"Forgive him he's shy." Said Ravana.

"Well he looks much better now. I take it you dressed him?" Samara asked.

"Of course, he has the most dreadful taste in clothes. You should have seen the things he tried to pick out. Dreadful."

The two circled around Thomas, like vultures inspecting him.

"He's mine." Ravana whispered under gritted teeth.

Regan shot her a glance. "He's yours? We'll see about that." She whispered back.

"No no no, my dear Regan. Thomas loves me." She said loud enough for everyone.

"He loves you!" Samara nearly shouted. "You've only just met."

"No it's true." Thomas stuttered. "I know I've only met her just last night, but I love her. She's been so kind to me, her father as well."

"Payment is in order ladies." Ravana grinned from ear to ear.

"He loves you? I don't believe it." Said Regan.

Thomas was confused about the conversation but he usually was when women were conversing together. To be honest he never really understood women.

Regan and Samara walked away in a huff.

"She cast a spell on him." Regan said.

"Oh, I know she did." Samara said.

"The look on his face was of a mindless obedient puppy dog"

"We have to give her our wands!"

"Oh no we don't, love spells don't count."

"Oh girls, don't forget our wager." Ravana called after them. "I want them by tonight."

Thomas was still confused. What wager he wondered?

Thomas looked at Ravana, "I said I love you, but I have nothing to give you but my love. I have no job, no money, nothing."

"I will talk to my father. He can give you a job. You're a strapping young man. What would like to do?"

"I have no idea; I've never actually had a job before."

"Captain of the guards I think. You may look like a farmhand but you do have royal blood in you. I'll talk to him tonight."

They returned to Ravana's castle, her home. Ravana went straight to her father. Thomas sat in the den.

"Did you find what you were looking for? The book you so desperately need." Ravana asked.

"No." Said The Prince flatly. "Have him come to my library at once."

"I will father, but first I have to talk to you about him. He loves me, he said so."

"He loves you?" The Prince showed concern, here the boy who had caused so much trouble for him was now a suitor for his daughter. "And do you love him?"

"I fancy him."

"Well now fancy, stop everything."

"I want to marry, to bear a child, to give you an heir."

"Interesting, yes I do want to carry on my lineage. I was upset I never had a son."

Ravana winced at the remark. "Anyway, he needs gainful employment. Can you get him job? I think he would be good in the guards."

"We'll see; first I need to talk to him."

Thomas showed up in The Prince's library, he was worried that he was not good enough for his daughter. He was worried The Prince would now tell him to go away, to never come back and to never darken his door. Thomas was a worrier.

"Thomas, come in. Have a drink, it is some of my best whiskey."

Thomas took the drink from him and took a sip. He took another to calm his nerves, and then another.

"Whoa, take it easy there, that's strong stuff.

"Sorry sir, I'm just a bit nervous."

"Don't worry son. You have nothing to fear, Ravana told me you love her and she likes you as well."

"I know it's all a bit sudden. I don't understand it myself but…"

"Don't worry, don't worry. The heart is a funny thing. You never know when love will hit you. It can strike without warning. Ravana's mother died when she was very young. I never had a son, and always wished I had. You could be like a son to me."

"Thank you, sir."

"Tell me what do you think of my library?"

"It's very impressive. I've only just recently learned how to read."

The Prince was astounded at Thomas's admission. "I have books of all sorts, I collect them. You say you just recently learned how to read? That's amazing to me."

"Yes sir, a very close friend taught me." Again Thomas left out the part of his friend being an ogre.

"Have you ever owned a book?" The Prince had been very careful not to reveal his desire for the book.

"Well kind of. My father left me a book in his belongings. It was in my back pocket when I was tossed off the boat."

"You didn't know what you had? Amazing." The Prince could barely contain himself. "This book is at the bottom of the sea now?"

"Yes, I'm sorry. I know how scarce books are."

The Prince let out laugh of relief. "That's ok, I have many books here. You're welcome to read them. Look at these authors, Shakespeare, Edgar Allan Poe, Chaucer, and Coleridge. Ah here's one of my favorites, the collected works of H.P. Lovecraft."

The names of the authors meant nothing to Thomas, he had never heard of them, and only a few weeks ago he was reading ogre children's books.

"I'm going to tell you a secret Thomas. I'm going to tell you something very few people know today. Hundreds of years ago, mankind was the only truly intelligent species on earth. There were large civilizations of cities, mankind pushed the limits of science, we even split the atom, the very fabric of what everything is made of."

Thomas had no idea what an atom was but he knew when to keep quiet.

"Then man began to dabble with the material of what man is made of, genes, the building blocks of humans and other animals. Man began to splice the genes and even create new races of sentient beings, which is why we have such foul bastardizations as ogres and melflings."

Thomas poured himself a drink, hardly believing the words that were being spoken.

"Then man went too far, they accidently created the dargon, originally created as a weapon of destruction for war, but the dargon turned on all mankind. The world was destroyed as these creatures devoured and multiplied. Everything was lost, civilization was laid down. Mankind went back to the dark ages."

"An incredible story." Thomas looked at him disbelief.

"It's not just a story it's history." The Prince looked at him with derision.

"Look here." The Prince took a book from his shelf and opened it to a picture. "This is a place called New York City, look how tall the buildings were. This a place called Moscow, Red Square. This is Beijing. Civilization was not only vast; mankind had built towers into the very sky."

"I'm sorry it just seems too much to take in." Thomas said.

"This city, the ground that you are standing on was once a great city called Auckland. It is one of the few lands not overcome by the dargon horde."

"Why are you telling me all this."

"I want you to be the son I never had. I knew your father, he fought in my Army, I feel like I owe you something."

"I hope I can live up to that."

"We need to find you a job Thomas, tomorrow report to the guards. Take this letter of appointment with you. You will be an officer."

"Thank you, sir."

"Take this book with you. The Cask of Amontillado, by Poe. I think you will enjoy."

Thomas took another drink and went off to bed. His head was heavy.

The Prince couldn't be happier, the book that risked his very life was lying at the bottom of the ocean, likely rotten away from the sea or swallowed by fish. The Prince couldn't be happier.

Chapter 12

Fighting with yourself

Yesterday, upon the stair, I met a man who wasn't there. He wasn't there again today, I wish, I wish he'd go away...

When I came home last night at three, The man was waiting there for me But when I looked around the hall, I couldn't see him there at all! Go away, go away, don't you come back any more! Go away, go away, and please don't slam the door...

Last night I saw upon the stair, A little man who wasn't there, He wasn't there again today Oh, how I wish he'd go away...

-Hughes Mearns, Antigonish

Thomas carried the note from The Prince appointing him to the guards. He was lost and trying to find the commander of the guard's office. Thomas walked down the stone arched hallways lined with guards in shiny black armor. The soldiers had an unusual blank stare which made Thomas nervous. Their eyes looked straight forward and paid no heed to him as he walked past them. They stood perfectly in row after row in a straight line along the hallways, each hallway seemed to look the same. He asked a guard outside a doorway where the commander was and was met with no answer, not even a blink. The hallway was quiet and each step he took echoed on the stone floor, announcing every move he made. Finally, he came upon a man walking the other way. The man was put out by Thomas stopping him, but he huffed and said that the commander's office was two halls down, in the middle. The man rushed off, a handful of papers in his hand.

He entered the office with hesitation feeling like a man about to meet his doom. A job is something he never desired. He loved living off the land, farming and hunting.

"What?" Was all the commander said, not even looking up from a handful of papers.

"Are you Major Arturas?"

"I am who I am. I'm here rotting away in a stone office, a prisoner, while a war wages on and ravages the country. The Eastern Army is no more and all I do is sit here signing papers."

"I know you, sir, you brought my father's body back to Greystone, we grew up together. I'm Thomas Kray."

The Major looked up from his paperwork, "I didn't even recognize you. You've changed in just a few short months."

"It's good to see you again sir."

"Good to see you as well. You've changed a lot; you have that look in your eye. You've seen combat."

"Yes sir, I've lost a good friend as well."

"Your father was a friend of mine. What brings you here?"

"The Prince has sent this letter of appointment for me. But with all due respects sir, I don't think I can be like one of those guards that line the hallways."

Major Arturas unfolded the paper and looked at. "You're friends with The Prince are you?"

"Not exactly." Thomas said. "I'm in love with his daughter and they took pity on me and took me into their home when I was homeless and cold."

"Thomas," Major Arturas hesitated and then spoke in a hushed tone. "I speak carefully lest I be called treasonous. Be careful around that man."

"He's been very kind to me so far."

"His kindness comes with a hefty price. His daughter is a ..." Major Arturas trailed off with his sentence.

"Is what sir?"

He shook his head, "Never mind, just be careful. There's something about them and I cannot put my finger on it. Something is wrong with him."

"I will, thank you. What of my posting though? What job will I be doing?"

"Don't worry about being a common guard. I will make you a lieutenant. You can be my aide for now. We'll see how you do."

"I won't let you down."

"Good. Now first order of business. Our scouts captured an ogre just two days ago."

"An ogre?"

"Yes the foul abomination is rotting in our dungeon now. I don't know what to do with him."

Thomas feared the worse, he knew it was Unkh. He didn't know what to do about it.

"The Prince wants a public execution. The ogre wasn't doing anything, but there have been many reports of one stealing livestock on the borders."

"What do you want me to do?" Thomas asked with trepidation.

"Tomorrow you can accompany me as we interrogate it. Be here at eight o'clock."

"Eight o'clock?" Thomas asked wondering what eight o'clock even meant."

Arturas chuckled. "We here in Storm Gap keep track of time. He took Thomas to the window and pointed to the clock tower. "Tomorrow morning when that small hand reaches the eight and the big hand reaches the twelve, be here. Thomas, tonight we should dine together, catch up on things, eat dinner. I have few friends here it would be good get together and have some fun."

"I would love that."

"Great, meet me here at sunset. We shall go out on the town."

Thomas walked back to The Prince's castle more perplexed than ever before. He had to do something for Unkh. But if anyone found out he was helping an ogre they would hang him as well.

Ravana greeted him at the door. "Darling we have to talk."

"Talk about what?"

"Well, I was in the bazaar today, looking at the most beautiful engagement rings."

"You mean, for marriage?"

"Of course that's what engagement rings are for! I swear I don't know what I see in you. You're handsome but not the brightest."

Thomas blushed. "I mean we just met, isn't marriage a little soon?"

"Are you saying you don't love me?"

"Well yes, I love you. I just not sure if we should get married so soon."

"You don't love me." Ravana wondered what was wrong, the spell was not strong enough. She had to make a stronger one.

"No, no. I love you. There's just something in the back of my head and I'm…confused."

"Well I bought the ring, you can pay me back later when you start getting paid."

"You bought a ring?"

"I have to have one if we're to get married. Look at the ring, isn't it beautiful?"

"Wow! You're already wearing it."

"I wanted you to see how it looked. It's not the same if you don't see it on my finger." Ravana talked to him like he was a child. He didn't seem to notice however; he was blind to the way she was treating him. "Like I said though, you can pay me back later. You will be making good money working for the guards. My father makes sure that the officers are paid well."

"How did you know I was made an officer?"

"Do you really think I would marry a simple guard?"

"No of course not."

"I have another little thing I have to tell you." Ravana said.

"What's that?"

"It's your beard, it really needs to come off."

"My beard is an essential part of my being. This beard has protected me in times of trouble. It's quite possible arrow proof." Thomas thought a minute, "No not really arrow proof perhaps, but arrows fear the beard and swerve to one side to avoid it."

Ravana looked at him as if he was crazy, he was joking of course but she didn't smile."

"We'll talk later. I have something I must do."

Ravana was perplexed, Thomas was resisting the notion of marriage. She had made another bet with Samara and Regan that Thomas would not marry her and now the stakes were higher. She didn't want to lose, she never loses. What she needed now was a stronger spell and she knew what she needed. Blood needed to be spilled. She strolled up the stairs and into her room. The pink candle, half melted still remained in its spot in the middle of the circle. She replaced it with black candle and two red ones. She rang the bell for her servant and a young girl promptly appeared at her door. She ordered the servant to the middle of the circle with merely a hand gesture. She took a knife from in between her breasts and thrust in the heart of the young maiden, gouging it out with the skill of a surgeon.

The girl fell lifeless to the floor like a used rag. Ravana held up the heart above her head and said another incantation.

Dark power,
Dark night,
Red heart for sacrifice,
Make Thomas forget his will,
Make him do all my bidding.

Ravana placed the heart in the center of the circle and smashed it with her foot. She looked down at the lifeless girl lying on the floor. She rang the bell again and this time an older man came to the door.

"Clean up this mess." She then went off and cleaned herself up.

She walked down stairs to find Thomas.

"Now darling, I was thinking. We should have a large engagement ceremony, but a small wedding."

"Yes of course. Small wedding. Just close family. I don't have family here so it will be just your friends and your father."

"I'm glad you see things my way."

"Of course, anything to please you. I will pay you back for the ring as soon as possible. I want to get you a nice band as well."

"We need to get a band for you as well."

"Of course, I like black bands."

"Don't be silly, you'll get a traditional gold band."

"Of course, I'm sorry. What was I thinking. A gold band is better. I need to go; I'm meeting a friend at sunset. He's from my town, Greystone."

"Well you have my permission." Ravana said.

"Thank you."

Thomas left the castle feeling very strange but looking forward to meeting with Arturas. Thomas stepped outside, it was getting dark already and there was a homeless man on the corner. Thomas looked at the man and was thankful for being taken in by The Prince, it could very well be him sitting on the ground hoping for a meal. Thomas didn't have much money but he gave some to the poor man and continued on his way to meet Arturas. Thomas passed the homeless man and he gave him a heartfelt thanks. Out of the darkness of the alley stepped the beast Gaap, steam escaped from his large nostrils and he breathed heavily. The homeless man screamed but was instantly silenced as he was dragged into the alleyway and devoured.

Thomas met Arturas in the same office as this morning, he was no out of his armor and in a better spirit.

"I hope you like drinking, Thomas. Follow me." He said with a smile.

The tavern was called the Lucky Dog, and the officers of the guard would hang out there. Arturas ordered whiskey for the both of them.

"Drink up, old friend. How about a toast."

"To friends lost." Thomas called out.

"To friends lost!" Arturas yelled and ordered four more.

Thomas took another drink and Arturas ordered downed both of his.

"My job is terrible and I hate being married, Thomas. I miss the single life."

"What's bad about the job?"

"It's boring." He said. "Nothing but paperwork, shuffle this, do this report. I miss the action of battle. Sure there was danger, but I miss that thrill."

"Aye, I know what you mean."

"Do you have any children?"

"Yes a son, love him to death. The only reason why I stay with my wife."

"Let's have another drink." Shouted Thomas.

"An excellent idea, my friend."

"You toast this time, Arturas."

"To the Guard!" Arturas shouted.

"To the Guard!" Shouted several other soldiers nearby.

"Let's take this party to a table, Thomas."

"Aye, to a table. I'm going to be married too." Said Thomas. "I was just engaged today."

"Hey ladies how are you doing." Arturas said to two passing young girls. "I love you." He said to the blonde who smiled back at him.

At the table Arturas pulled out a packet of blue powder and laid it out on the table. He took his knife and made it into a neat line. Arturas took out a federation bill and rolled into a tube and snorted half the line of the fine blue powdery substance then offered the bill to Thomas.

"What is that?"

"It's a drug, it's called krush, makes you high and feel strong. Makes you feel like you can do anything."

"And you snort this up your nose?"

"Try it."

"No thanks, I got water up my nose once and sneezed for an hour."

Arturas laughed. "Suit yourself." He said, and snorted the rest of the line.

Thomas had never heard of krush but he knew somehow it was wrong. Arturas rubbed his nose vigorously trying not to sneeze, his eyes went red and so did his face. A somewhat demonic look came over his face and he smiled.

"Evil Arturas has come out to play." He said. "Excuse me Thomas, I'm going to go talk to that chubby little blonde girl that smiled at me."

Thomas got up from the table and staggered back to the castle. He had too much to drink and was in whirlwind about the whole events of the day. He was engaged to be married and he didn't remember proposing. His old friend from Greystone was here with a family and now cheating, or attempting to cheat on his wife, and his friend Unkh was locked up and in a dungeon. Things couldn't be worse.

The next morning Thomas showed up at Arturas's office promptly at eight, just as he was told.

His head hurt, throbbed as a matter of fact. He had slept restlessly. Arturas was ten minutes late and looked just as bad from the wear and tear of too much drink.

"Let's go interrogate this abominable ogre. I will show you how it's done."

They walked together down to the dungeon below. There were other creatures there, a melfling was locked up in a cage and a goblin laughed maniacally chained to a wall. Arturas opened the door to a cell and the ogre looked up. Just as Thomas had feared it was Unkh. Unkh's eyes showed confusion and Thomas motioned with his hand not to say anything. Arturas kicked Unkh with a ferocity that made the ogre reel, massive chains held Unkh pinned to the ground and unable to fight back.

Arturas showed no fear for the ogre and looked at him straight. "What's your name, ogre?"

Unkh was indignant. He looked Arturas up and down and smiled, not saying a word.

"Oh, you're a tough guy." Arturas kicked him again, this time in the stomach.

Thomas felt helpless, he couldn't look Unkh in the eye and cringed each time Arturas kicked him.

Unkh winced, "Unkh." He said.

Arturas kicked him again in the same place, "I said tell me your name."

"Unkh, my name is Unkh Headknocker."

"Your name is Unkh? I'm sorry but that is the dumbest name I've ever heard. Unkh is the sound I make when I stub my toe."

"Headknocker is my last name, perhaps you would like to find out what that name means."

"I see, you're a funny ogre. You like to joke when you're chained to the floor and being kicked."

"Do your worst." Unkh said.

Arturas punched him in the face but this time Thomas was sure it hurt Arturas's hand more than it did Unkh. Unkh just smiled back.

"Do you have a family?" Arturas asked, shaking his hand.

"Yes, I have a family. I have a wife and two ogre children."

"A boy and a girl?"

"Two boys." Unkh said.

Thomas wondered if Unkh had children that he never mentioned or he was lying now but he kept silent.

"Two boys, I see that the ogre gods have honored you, it is a blessing to have two boys."

"I worship no gods." Unkh said flatly.

"A heathen ogre. Tell me about your sons."

Unkh lowered his head.

"I see, I hit a soft spot. You love your children, that's plain to see. You miss them being locked up here. You miss playing with them, doing ogre games and eating ogre meals made by your ogre wife. I bet you can smell that roast mutton on the stove right now, the meal that your wife used to cook especially for you. But now your children are fatherless, you're locked up here in this filthy dungeon. This place is filthy, it's damp, and it's cold at night. You have nothing, no freedom, bad food, you're chained to the floor and you have nothing to look at.

No sunshine, no trees, no nothing. You're in a desperate situation my big ogre friend."

"What do you want?" Unkh asked.

"I want to know why you were captured gallivanting around on the border. Are you some ogre scout sent out to spy on our lands? Are the ogres planning an attack on Storm Gap?"

"I will tell you nothing."

"Listen, you are in a dire straight. I can make you a deal. Tell me what you and your ogre army are up to and I will spare your life. I will set you free and you can go back home to your fat ogre wife and your two children. This is your choice, to be with your family, or stay locked up here, never to see the light of day again. This your choice, tell me what the ogre army is up to and be free with your family, or keep your mouth shut and rot in this filthy dungeon."

Unkh said nothing. He lowered his head again.

Arturas went to kick him again but Thomas stopped him. "Let me talk to him a second sir, just a minute."

Arturas nodded his head with approval.

Thomas leaned over and whispered in Unkh's ear. "I will get you out of here, just tell him that you were just stealing sheep and nothing else."

Unkh nodded.

"Do you really have a family?"

Unkh whispered back, "Of course not, I'm a bachelor for life."

Thomas smiled.

Unkh looked at Arturas, "I was just stealing sheep, nothing else. There's no ogre invasion or attack or anything else."

Arturas shook his head, "I don't believe you ogre." He kicked him again.

Thomas leaned over again and whispered, "Just tell him there's an attack, then he'll set you free. Make it believable though."

"There's going to be an attack in one week. You're correct. I'm scout for the army."

"I knew it."

"Let's go Thomas, we have to alert everyone."

They left the cell and began walking up the stairs.

"What did you whisper in his ear, Thomas?"

"Umm, I told him you were planning to cut off his hands."

"Excellent work."

"When will you set him free?"

"Set him free? Are you joking, I'm not setting him free. Unless chopping his head off and dumping his body in the river is what you mean by setting him free, then yes I'm setting him free." Arturas laughed.

"But you said you would set him free."

"I say a lot of things; the ogre is an enemy scout who was laying plans for an attack. Do you really think we would set him free?"

"No, I guess not. Sorry I'm being stupid."

"You'll get the hang of this, don't worry. I'm just glad I could get away from my office for a while."

"I have more business to attend to, I have to punish a guard go for being late."

"Being late."

"Yes punctuality is very important for the guards, you have to maintain discipline with them or they will get out of line easily."

Thomas looked at him bewildered, Arturas himself was late this morning. This was not the man he used to know growing up in Greystone. Again he said nothing. Thomas was beginning to have a heavy heart from saying nothing.

"You can leave at five, Thomas. We should go to the Lucky Dog again soon."

"The Lucky Dog again, of course, I had a great time last night."

Five o'clock rolled around at a snail's pace. Thomas had nothing other work but worry about what he was going to do about Unkh. If he were to set him free there would be no doubt in his mind he would be risking his life. If he did anything he could be caught. Now his heart was getting heavy from doing nothing as well.

Thomas went home. Home? Now he was calling that odd castle his home. He stood outside the door of the castle and looked up, stone demons lined the ramparts. When he entered Ravana was there with the other two girls that he had met the day before. The other two girls made Thomas feel awkward.

"We heard that you two are getting married." Samarra said.

"Is that true?" Regan asked.

"Of course it's true, tell them Thomas." Ravana demanded.

"Yes, were getting married, we haven't set a date yet."

"This Saturday." Ravana said.

In the port of Storm Gap, Aurella and Moshki stepped off the Pale Witch and finally were able to step on shore. It was not an easy trip for them. On the return trip the sailors had begun to make unwanted advances toward her. Without the protection of Thomas by her side they would make rude comments to her, thankfully Captain Dmitri punished a couple and threatened lashings for anyone who touched her. She would sit in her cabin and cry afraid to go outside. They more relieved than ever to step on solid ground and no immediate desires to step foot on the ship soon.

"I'm hungry." Said Moshki. "Hungry for real food, not stale biscuits and hard cheese. I want something good."

"You're always hungry." Laughed Aurella.

"We haven't had real food for months."

"Do you think he's here, Moshki? Do you think he's still alive?"

"I feel that he's alive as well, my dear."

"What do the bones say?"

Moshki pulled out his leather pouch and crouched down on the dock. He emptied the small fragments of bones into his left hand and tossed them against a wooden beam.

"He's alive, they tell me. But he's in deep trouble, he needs our help."

Aurella let out a sigh of relief. "That's great news, I knew he was alright."

"Well let's not waste time, let's find him."

"Where should we start?"

"Let's start in the middle and work our way around."

A small funny man, very skinny and frail approached Moshki and Aurella. He was old with a long white beard and he wore a turban on his head. He was hunched over and carried a crooked walking stick. He was dressed in the most colorful robe, with more colors than a rainbow. He was a salesman in the bazaar by the docks.

"Madame, come and look at my goods. Come inside and look in my shop, I have many magical and useful things."

"No thank you." Moshki said.

Aurella started looking through the window at the man's store.

"Don't look." Moshki whispered to her, "Once you look he will pester you more."

But it was too late, Aurella was already opening the door. Moshki let out a sigh of resignation.

"My name is Glove; this is my shop. Glove's Magical and Useful Things. I will make you a very good deal, my friend."

"What do you have that is magical?"

"I have this magic potion; the drinker will instantly fall in love with you. This potion was made by the lady of the castle herself, Ravana."

"No thank you. I already have someone who loves me." Aurella said and turned to leave.

"Wait, don't go. I have many other magical things. Look I have a ring; the wearer will have the ability to walk in the shadows undetected."

"I don't need anything like that either." Aurella turned to walk away again.

"Wait, I have this compass. It is magical, the person you love will always be able to find you with this compass."

Aurella looked at the compass with interest and Glove knew he had found his sale by the look in her eyes. The compass was made of brass, with many dials and buttons. It opened and closed with hinges and was the size of a hand. There was writing along sides in an unknown language.

"Can I find the one I love with this compass?"

"Alas, no Madame. It can only be set to you."

"I can't use it then." She said.

"Wait, wait. If you find your love, give this to him and he will always be able to find again."

"Hmm." She pondered. "How much is it?"

"Since you are my first customer of the day, I will give you a special offer. Only two gold pieces."

"That's too much." Moshki said, taking over the conversation. "One half a gold piece"

"What, you speak for her, melfling?"

"I'm her protector."

"You're too small to be her protector." Glove asked.

"I protect her from con artists." Moshki retorted.

"This compass is finely crafted, it was made in the forges beneath castle Arken, and then infused with magic by the great wizard Michael of Perth himself. One and half gold pieces, and I am losing money with that deal."

"One gold piece." Said Moshki.

"You are robbing me; I have twelve children at home that need to eat. One gold, twenty silver."

"You're too old for children old man."

"I'll take it." Said Aurella.

"Very good, you are getting a steal, my friend. Shall I wrap it for you?"

"That's ok." She said handing him the gold and silver.

"Before you leave I have to set the compass to you, and only." Glove took the compass and pointed it at her, pressing a switch on the side, he then broke the switch off the compass and handed it to her.

"That's it?" She asked.

"That's it my friend. It will always point to you, let me demonstrate. Watch."

Glove walked around her in a circle, the needle followed Aurella around.

"Wonderful!" She said.

"I hope it stays working." Moshki said pessimistically.

Glove smiled, "I guarantee everything in my store. If it doesn't work, just bring it back to me and I will give you a replacement."

They left the bazaar and went to the park in the middle of the city, it was beautiful with lush trees and park benches. An old woman walked passed them.

"Abomination." She said giving Moshki an evil look.

Aurella became furious and got up into the woman's face.

"You call him an abomination? This melfling has saved my life, he has given me comfort in times of trouble, and he has helped me the worst of times. If he is an abomination then what are you, hypocrite!"

Moshki motioned to stop her, he was used to being ridiculed but he was never called an abomination. But Aurella was just getting started.

"He's the kindest creature, he is loyal and brave. He has looked death in the eye and joked about it. He's more human than most humans I know."

The woman shrunk at Aurella's unleashed tirade and turned red in the face. She gave Moshki the evil eye and ran off.

Moshki laughed, "I guess they don't get many melflings in this two-bit town."

"Well they better get used to it."

"I care more for food right now than that old woman's narrow minded sentiments. There's a vendor over there selling my favorite. Meat on a stick."

They sat down on a bench on began eating their food.

"That woman still has me fuming."

"Who ever invented meat on a stick was a genius." Moshki said.

"She really got my blood boiling."

"Now cheese on a stick would be good too."

"Doesn't it bother you she called you that?"

Moshki put his stick down for a second and pondered. "I've never been called an abomination before. Thief. Bum. Rogue. Never an abomination, I don't know why, but I'll live with it."

"I don't want you to live with that, Moshki."

"My, what an ugly castle." Moshki said.

"Stop trying to change the subject."

"No, look at the castle. Normally castles are beautiful. That looks sinister. There are demon statues staring down at us."

Aurella pondered at the castle, it was black with tall towers but not very big. It was a cool evening and she saw Thomas coming out of the castle, he was holding the hand of another girl.She was horrified and Moshki saw it too. They were both speechless, and Aurella hung her head and cried.

"Come Moshki. He forgot about me."

Moshki threw his food down, for once he had lost his appetite. He felt horrible as well, all the faith they had in finding him was destroyed. He couldn't look and they walked away. Everything they had hoped for was dashed away in a single moment. Aurella couldn't stop crying, she was completely heartbroken.

"What now, Moshki? What will we do?"

"I have enough money to sail back.I know the thought of being on the sea again is troublesome, but I know of nothing else."

"Ok then, we leave as soon as possible. Here, take his bag of his belongings and make sure that he gets it."

"I will. I'll make sure that he gets it."

Thomas came home by himself, Samara, Ravana, and Regan all stayed out. It was girl's night they said. He was a bit relieved though. He found it tiresome to be with them and he wondered for the first time why did he love Ravana? She had never said she loved him back. He tried to put the thought aside. He walked up the stairs, and he looked up and saw a man on the stair. It was late, after midnight. The man on the stair was not The Prince. He suddenly realized the man was wearing his old clothes. He started walking up the stairs.

"You there. Who are you?"

The man didn't answer and had maniacal look on his face. A look of anger and with sudden horror Thomas realized it was himself. A mirror image. With every step he took, his mirror image did the same. The only difference was the look of anger, the furrowed brow, and his clenched fists. And of course the clothes, Thomas was wearing the new clothes the Ravana bought him. This man, this person, this thing had the daring to wear his old clothes.

"Why are you wearing my old clothes? What business do you have here?"

Again he did not answer. Thomas took a step up, his double took a step down. Thomas could see the anger in his face. His own face? They stepped closer and closer and Thomas knew that there was going to be trouble. They got within a few steps of each other, standing in the middle of the stair case. With ferocity his double leapt him like a pouncing leopard. They tumbled, hitting every step going down. They landed at the bottom and Thomas punched him hard in the face. He didn't know who this joker was, impersonating him and attacking him. But he was going to finish him off. He hit him hard again and again. He was winning, and he would teach this duplicate a lesson. Thomas got up and he was breathing hard, his fists were bloody and scratched. He received several blows to the stomach and several bruises falling down the stairs but he was triumphant.

"I'm asking again, who are you and what do you want?"

Thomas looked down to where they had fought, and the man was gone. Had he escaped? He looked around and there was no sign of him. He had not heard the sounds of a closing door or the footsteps of him leaving. Had it been a dream. His bruises and bloody knuckles said differently. Impossible he thought. He brushed himself off but with a grasping fright, he was wearing his old clothes. He began to shake and feel as if he was going insane.

He climbed the stairs with pain every step of the way. He wanted nothing more than to lie in his bed and go to sleep. He was surprised to see that on his bed was a bag, a leather pouch. In the pouch was gold, gems and the book and suddenly he remembered Aurella and how much he loved her. There was the book that only months before he could not read. He opened the book to no particular page.

It read: The Gospel According to John,
In the beginning was the Word,
And the word was with God, and the Word was God,
The same was in the beginning with God.
All things were made by him; and without him was not

> any thing made that was made.
> In him was life; and the life was the light of men.
> And the light shineth in darkness; and the darkness comprehended it not.

He put the book down back on the bed. Thomas still felt as if he was going insane, but he knew what he had to do. Sleep would come later. Ten minutes later he was in Arturas's office, he found them no problem.

"I am crazy." Thomas said to himself. "Tomorrow at this time I will be locked up."

There was a guard at the door leading to the dungeon, Thomas walked up to him like he was supposed to be there.

"Step aside guard, I've orders to prepare the ogre for execution."

"I wasn't made aware of this sir." He said sternly.

Thomas got into his face, "Why do you think I'm here soldier. Do you think I'm here to take the ogre out to dinner? Why do you think I have these keys?"

"No sir, I'm sorry."

"Step aside." Thomas ordered and this time the guard complied.

Thomas opened the door to Unkh's cell. He was lying asleep and snoring. Thomas knelt down and shook him.

"Wake up, you ugly old beast."

Unkh stirred and nearly hit Thomas.

"Thomas!"

"Shhh, be quiet."

"Are you breaking me out?"

"Yes."

"Great, what's your plan?"

"The plan is to walk you out the front door."

"Are you crazy?"

"Yes, I'm pretty sure I am. I had a fist fight with myself earlier, and I'm not sure if I won or lost."

Unkh merely looked at him.

"Look, I'm going to act like I'm taking you to be executed, it was Arturas's plan all along. I'm going to leave you shackled. We're going to walk out that front door and just keep walking. It's late but with any hope everyone will be asleep."

They walked up the stairs with Unkh still in chains as they walked passed the guard.

"Don't try anything ogre, you will regret any effort to escape."

Thomas gave the guard a nod and they walked out into the streets to the gates of Storm Gap.

"I can't believe that worked." Unkh said.

"Me either, now go back home and try to keep low this time."

Thomas unlocked the chains and they said goodbye.

"I hope to see again ogre, just not locked up next time."

"I owe you human, we will see each other again."

Thomas went back in town, he was very tired and didn't want to return to Ravana's home. He slept that night in some fishing nets near the docks.

Chapter 13

Into the Abyss

"When Thiye ruled Hjemur Came strangers riding there, And three were dark and one was gold, And one like frost was fair. Fair was she, and fatal as fair, And cursed who gave her ear; Now men are few and wolves are more, And the Winter drawing near."

- From "Gate of Ivrel" by C.J. Cherryh

Thomas woke up at dawn after very little sleep. He was sore from the fight and only one thought came to his mind, to find Aurella. He had to tell her how much he loved her. His father's book was in his pocket and he took it out.

Take unto you the whole armor of God, that ye may be able to withstand in the evil day, and done all, to stand.

He had no armor he thought. He had nothing. Is this what his father had fought for? For this book he laid down his life and risked everything. He stuck the book back in his pocket. Aurella and Moshki were walking up the dock. This was his chance and he ran to her.

"Aurella!" He called.

She stopped but it was not what he expected, there were tears in her eyes.

"You said you loved me and that you would marry me and we would always be together." She sobbed.

"I do love you."

"Then why were you with that girl."

"I... I don't know why. It wasn't me you have to believe me."

"It wasn't you? Was it your twin then?"

"No, I mean I wasn't myself, I was under some sort of magic, you must believe me."

"I see, that girl cast a spell on you and forced you to hold her hand."

"Well, in a word, yes."

"I don't believe you."

Moshki was silent the whole time and eyed Thomas suspiciously. He looked as if he had been betrayed as well. He tapped his foot and then he had a ponderous look about him, stroking his whiskers thoughtfully.

"Prove that you love me."

Thomas stepped forward and cupped her face, kissing her on the lips.

Moshki knelt down and once more got out his bag of bones and them on the planks of the dock. "He tells the truth miss Aurella. It's why he's in trouble as the bones said before."

Aurella softened in his embrace. "If you love me be here tomorrow, we're sailing once more for Trilliane. We just bought our passage."

"I swear I will be here. I just have to go back and get my things." Thomas dreaded going back into that castle but he had to get his father's belongings. Thomas began to walk back.

"Wait Thomas. I have something for you."

Aurella held out the brass compass for him.

"What is it?"

"It's a magic compass, you can find me wherever I am, the needle will point only to me. If you can't find me, use this."

"Thomas took the compass. "This really works?"

"I hope so, at least a man named Glove told me it work."

"Well you have to trust someone named Glove, I will keep it with me always."

Ravana, Samara, and Regan were in the bazaar. They had been shopping for the wedding. Ravana had picked out all types of decorations and her wedding gown.

"I will look fabulous in this dress." She told the others.

"Isn't that your man down on the docks?" Samara asked.

"Who Thomas?"

"Well, yes. Down there on the pier talking to another girl and of all things a melfling."

"He's kissing her." Chimed in Regan.

"I think someone's little spell didn't hold and owes us something big." Samara said.

Ravana was fuming. She stood there looking at Thomas holding another girl and was in total disbelief. "How could he!" She said aloud.

"He's completely betrayed you." Said Regan.

"Well he's going to pay for this! Just wait till I tell my father." Ravana stormed off with Samara and Regan close behind.

Thomas returned to the castle at dusk, there was an eerie light as the sun set down over the city. He had found a place to go back to sleep, he woke up fitfully near in an alley near a tavern. His first thought was of Aurella and he wondered how he could have possibly forgotten her. His next thought was if Unkh got out safely and if anyone had noticed he was gone. There had been no alarms. Ogres are not hard to track, they leave footprints as big as an elephant.

Thomas crept into the castle as soundlessly as possible and walked up the stairs, thankful his double was not at the top to fight again. He snuck into his room and was surprised that Ravana was there waiting for him.

"Where have you been, Thomas?"

"Look Ravana, there's something have to tell you."

"Oh I think you have plenty to tell me."

"I don't love you, I don't want to get married."

"I see, that's how you treat me."

"I'm sorry but I really don't think you love me either. You really just want the ring, not the marriage."

"Where did you get this?" She asked holding up the bag of gold and jewels.

"My father left them to me and Aurella made sure I got them back."

"You're funny. I mean nothing to you. I saw you kissing that girl on the pier this morning."

"Yes, I love her. Not you."

"Guards!" She screamed at the top of her lungs.

Guards? Wondered Thomas. What were guards doing here? Ravana grabbed the top her blouse and ripped it, putting a scratch across her chest with her fingernails. The guards burst in through the door.

"Arrest him!" She commanded, "He has accosted me. Look at what he did to me."

The guards didn't even talk to him, they grabbed him threw him down to the ground, placing him in shackles. They dragged him down the stairs, Thomas would have walked if they would have let him, but again he got to feel every step hit his body.

Ravana called after him. "I'll be keeping this bag, loser. You came with nothing and you leave with nothing. You will never have anything because you are a loser. Good luck, I hope they don't chop off your head."

The guards dragged him through the street and threw him in the very dungeon cell that Unkh had occupied just last night. When he noticed, he knew he was in trouble. Did they know it was him?

Arturas came into the cell, Thomas was laying on the floor still in shackles. Thomas looked at him thinking for a brief moment that he was here to help him, they were friends.

"Funny thing Thomas. A very funny thing happened earlier this morning. As you can tell by looking around in this cell there isn't an ogre here. You see… were missing an ogre, but that's not the funny part, the funny part is that someone escorted the prisoner right through the front door."

Thomas was bruised and realized Arturas wasn't there to help him.

"I'm a straight shooter Thomas, you know that. I call things like I see them. The guard last night said that a man led the ogre out, in shackles but there were no orders to have him moved."

Thomas knew where this was going. "I see, and tell me what you think."

"I think you let an ogre loose, the guard says it was a man fitting your description."

"You would think right but I had my reasons. That ogre was no threat to you or anyone else. You were going to have him killed."

"He was going to be executed because he's an ogre."

"The ogre was my friend. He saved me months ago, if not for him I would have never made it here, and froze during the winter."

"So you admit to letting him go."

"I do, like I said. He's good."

"I have no choice; you've tied my hands on this one."

"So our friendship means nothing to you? We grew up together."

"I'm a straight shooter." He repeated the phrase. It was ironic, he was anything but a straight a straight shooter and his repeating it made it sound like he was only trying to convince himself. "We were drinking buddies for a time, that's it. I would have you executed myself but The Prince has something special for you."

"You told me to stay clear of The Prince. Now you're turning me over to him."

"I'm a straight shooter."

Arturas left the cell without as much as a nod. Straight shooter, if there was ever a straight shooter it wasn't Arturas. Thomas had looked the other way over his drug use and hypocrisy because they were friends, now he regretted it. Thomas realized that he missed sailing with Aurella and he knew she would never forgive him now; the compass was seized along with what little else he had.

Thomas languished in the cell for a week until the guards came and got him. He was led back to The Prince's castle in chains. Ravana was not there when he got there which surprised him, she was a spiteful woman and he figured she would want to be there to gloat. He was led upstairs to the library where The Prince was waiting for him and the guards dumped him like garbage onto the floor. The Prince looked down at him.

"Brutal men. Please sit down in a chair, let me pour you a drink." Said The Prince.

Thomas was still chained but took the drink from him. Thomas looked at it before taking a sip, it could possibly be poisoned but what difference did it make. Thomas was resigned to his fate, knowing that his fate was most certain death. He might as well make the best of it. He gulped the drink down.

"Here, let's get those ridiculous chains off of you. Here, have another drink."

Thomas was getting drowsy. On the table in a corner was the compass that Aurella gave him along with the book and some of his other belongings. Behind the table there was something else, something that caused him great confusion.

"That's my father's sword in the corner." Thomas said.

The Prince glanced over in the corner. "So it is." He said as a matter of fact.

"How did you come by my father's sword? I lost it in battle months ago."

The Prince ignored the question. "Thomas, I'm going to tell you some things, some things that few people know."

Not this again Thomas thought. "You already told me the history of the world."

The Prince laughed. "No, no, Thomas. This a tale of the history of me. A far more interesting story in my opinion."

Thomas grimaced at his arrogance.

"Do you know my real name Thomas?" The Prince hesitated. "No of course you don't." He chuckled. "No one alive knows my real name, not even my daughter. I don't know why I ask that question every time. It's just something I do."

"So what is your real name?"

"Zahar. My name is Zahar, it means poison in an ancient tongue. My mother gave me the name; she was she was a beautiful woman who dabbled in the old languages. She had a thirst for knowledge, which she passed on to me. She taught me to read, and gave me a thirst for knowledge."

Thomas realized that Zahar's biggest admirer was himself. His continuous pontificating was wearing on him, and he was getting even sleepier. He knew for sure that The Prince had drugged his drink but somehow he didn't care. All was lost, he lost Aurella and the desire to keep living was slipping from his soul.

"I searched the world for knowledge, for more books. Risking attacks from dargons and other vile abominations. I stumbled on a great and wondrous book."

"You already told me about the history book."

"Don't interrupt me. No, this was a far better book, entitled The Lexicon of Baphomet. The author of the book is by an unknown man named Grundle de Octivo. Nothing else is known about him, there is no mention of him in any history books. But what's interesting is, who he cited as the co-author of the book. You'll never guess who it was."

"No sir, I couldn't and honestly I don't give a damn."

"Well now, tsk tsk. Let's not get irritable. Hear me out, this is where it gets interesting. Grundle cited the co-author as none other than Satan. Now mind you, I have no idea whether Grundle received some sort of undivine inspiration, like a prophet of the Devil.... or the Devil himself sat next to him guiding his words. Either way, the thought of it is fascinating and I have no doubts in my mind that Satan guided Grundle's writing and of the book's authenticity. I came upon this book high up in a mountain in an unholy temple long abandoned and ravaged by time but the book remained unharmed, although yellowed by time. You should have seen the temple, Thomas. It was beautiful and ugly at the same time. It was my inspiration for my own asylum I keep beneath this castle."

The glass slipped from Thomas's hand and broke on the floor. His mind was numb and he could no longer feel his body.

"I poured over the book and studied it day and night. This book opened the secrets to summoning demons of the foulest nature."

"Why?" Asked Thomas.

"Why what?"

"Why would you want to summon up demons from Hell?"

"For power of course. They do my bidding. Not to mention, there were other great arcane secrets unlocked from the Lexicon of Baphomet, it has given me the inability to age. I found that book over two hundred years ago."

"Is your story over? If so, I would just like to pass out now, thank you."

"My story is not quite over, but your story is about to end I'm afraid. You see tomorrow I will summon Baphomet. The great dragon. The conclusion of my long study, my life's work. And you play the biggest role in that part. Congratulations."

"You haven't told me how you have my father's sword."

"Well, you see I've been tracking you for some time. The book your father bequeathed to you is a holy book, something that would destroy my power. My way of life especially if other people read and it caught on. The only copy of the book was at the citadel. And now a religion has been spreading like a virus through this country even without that book, its existence could only threaten it more. I commissioned your father to get the holy book. But he betrayed me, he read the damned thing."

"I read some of it too."

"Yes, that's why you are the part of my ceremony tomorrow morning. And now that's the end of my story young one."

Thomas collapsed to the floor.

Ravana sauntered into her father's library looking for him, she knew that her father was talking to Thomas but she was surprised that they were not there. She saw Thomas's stuff in the corner, saw the sword and what she deemed as junk with the other things. She looked at the sword, and saw the Kray name on the hilt. She realized it belonged to Thomas and she picked it up to look over.

"This could sell for a pretty penny." She said out loud to herself.

She carefully wrapped it in a sheet and carried it out with both arms. She could barely lift it but she managed to get it downstairs and into the street. She pulled her cloak around her and covered her face with her hood. She made several turns on through Storm Gap and finally ended up at Dean Alley, a fairly nice part of the city. She knocked on the door of Arturas's house. She barely knew him but she knew that he would be interested in Thomas's sword.

"I'm surprised to see you here. What interest do you have in seeing me?"

"Trust me it's not about Thomas. He can rot in that dungeon for all I care."

"Then what brings you here?" Arturas asked.

"I have something that may interest you."

"Something that interests me?"

Ravana unwrapped Thomas's sword and showed it to him.

"I know you like swords, this belonged to Thomas. I want to get rid of it."

Arturas looked at the sword with an eager eye.

"I can't afford the sword right now." Arturas said and began to shut the door. "Besides it has his family name on it."

"Wait, you can get an engraver to polish it out, it's very valuable. I will sell it for 3500 silver just to be rid of it."

"3500? It's worth five times that."

"I know but like I said, I want to be rid of it. I don't want his memory around and a poor girl has to survive."

"Poor? You jest. You're not poor but I will take it off your hands."

Arturas gave Ravana the money, and he salivated over the sword. It was a beautiful piece of work.

The next morning Arturas did his usual, he shaved and put on his work clothes. He kissed his wife good bye and rustled his son's hair as he left. Arturas took the sword with him, thinking he would take a smith later to get the name taken off. He packed his lunch as usual in a knapsack, but he also packed a long piece of rope that he used to always take with him when he went out on patrols. He then walked to work taking his usual route.

In a dark office Arturas was sitting at his desk. He looked down at the papers and the blue line of the drug that he loved. He sucked up the line through a colorful glass tube and sneezed. He took a drink from the bottle of whisky in his drawer, and then he took a piece of rope that he brought with him that morning and made a hasty noose and hung the rope from the ceiling. He stepped onto his desk, slipped the noose around his neck and with quiet resignation took a step from his desk, he would close his eyes forevermore. It was unheroic and tragic. He kicked his legs, and grabbed at his neck in a desperate last minute he had a change of mind. His swayed back and forth as he kicked but he was far too far to reach his desk. It would be several days before anyone found his body. At his funeral several days later his wife and son were the only attendees, she didn't cry and after the final shovel load of dirt filled his grave she went home.

Thomas hanging upside down over the chasm the smell of Sulphur burning his lungs and throat. The Prince smiling maniacally up at him and his predicament.

"You're pathetic."

The Prince let him down to the floor but he was still bound.

"Time to meet the dragon." Zahar said.

Thomas heard a thunderous roar from the chasm in the ground. Smoke and fire started streaming up from the hole. For the first time Thomas felt real terror. Horror. A claw reached up from the chasm and gripped the edge. The dragon was the size of a house and Thomas was in awe at how beautiful he was. Silver scales lined every part of its body except his face which as black as a murderer's soul. The scales glistened and lit up with colors like the rainbow. Thomas thought he was going crazy but the dragon smiled a wicked grin. His tongue flicked out and in like a snake and he hissed.

The dragon lumbered into the chamber and took a seat on a massive throne and Zahar sat down at the dragon's right hand. The dragon placed his claw and rested on Zahar's head like he was some sort of pet. Thomas wanted to look away but he couldn't. Zahar grinned like a child at a puppet show. The dragon chuckled and a small lick of flame shot from its nostrils.

"I will devour your bones and wear your intestines like a hat." The dragon said, speaking for the first time.

Thomas closed his eyes and the words came into his mind. The words he read this morning, Take up the whole armor of God.

"You have no power over me." Thomas said, barely audible.

The dragon let out a roar of laughter. "What did you say? You impudent little thing. Do you know who I am?"

"You have no power over me." Thomas said again, only louder and with confidence.

The dragon stopped laughing and a look of dismay came over his face. Puffs of steam came out of his mouth and he looked down at Zahar. The look of dismay turned to anger and his grip on Zahar's head tightened. The smile suddenly left Zahar's face as blood trickled down the sides of his face. The dragon popped Zahar's skull like an over ripe melon and his now limp body fell to the stone floor with a thud.

The dragon got up from the throne and walked over to Thomas, the dragon was face to face with Thomas. Only inches away, one snort of fire would vaporize Thomas. The dragon did nothing, he crawled back down the chasm from where he came.

Thomas got up, his legs and arms still bound. A ceremonial knife was sitting on the throne and Thomas was able to cut himself free. He staggered up the stairs and found his way back into Zahar's library. His belongings were still in the corner. He grabbed the holy book and the compass. The sword was missing, but he hardly cared. His wrists and ankles were raw and bleeding. He staggered out into the street and fell to his knees. And at that moment, that brief fleeting moment it felt as if time froze and it began to rain. Thomas began to shed tears, he cried for his father he barely knew, he cried for his dead mother, he cried for his lost friend and his lost love.

Thomas took out the knife, kneeling in the dirt and grasping it with both hands, his body heaving. He placed the knife to his belly, working up the courage to thrust the knife through and to end the pain that he felt in his heart. He was a failure. He struggled, his body trembled, he began to take fast deep breaths. He then looked down at his hands, and dropped the knife and walked away.

A few days later, Thomas walked along the dock. The Pale Witch was moored at the end. Thomas was happy to see the familiar ship. The sleek black wooden hull and the square sails, with a blue flag of four red stars flying in the rear reminded him of a better time. Thomas chewed absent mindedly on a piece of chicken roasted on a stick that he bought in the bazaar with his last bit of money. He had been waiting for the Pale Witch to come into port with anxious anxiety, sleeping on the beach underneath an overturned rowboat. Captain Dmitri was on the deck barking orders to his men when Thomas walked up.

"What brings you here, laddie?" Dmitri asked. "I dropped yer girl off in this port a few days ago, she's been looking for you something fierce."

"I missed her, now I'm going to go find her. I have no money to book passage with you. I was hoping you could use an extra hand. I have some experience on a boat."

"I can always use an extra hand, but the work will be harder this time around and you won't get the deluxe accommodations you had last time. You sleep with the crew with everyone else, in a hammock. Works starts at sunrise."

"Agreed then. I don't have much in the way of choices."

"Alright then. Where are you heading?"

Thomas pulled the bronze compass from his pocket and flipped it open. The dial spun around three times, then settled on a northerly direction. Thomas read the needle.

"That way." He said.

The breeze picked up and the sails opened as the sailors began to sing their songs once more.

When you find your true love you don't give up, you keep going till you find her. You pick yourself up again and again, while shallow people try to push you down. You fight the good fight. You fight on while smug cowards sit comfortably at home and speak ill of the fallen soldier. You try not to forget the faces of your fallen friends.

A red headed girl no more than five years old sat on rock, in rapt attention, it looked as if a noodle factory exploded on her head and she bounced her hair around nonchalantly in the cool autumn breeze. A blonde, moppet headed, boy no more than six sat next to her. They sat by the sea shore and the waves crashed with a regular thunder every five minutes. They held each other's hands like a brother and sister should. The sun was setting and a scarlet sky let them know that there was fair weather ahead. A sheep bahed in disgruntlement nearby, in disapproving condemnation. No one was sure what the sheep was disapproving, but it was not good, maybe it was the story papa had just told but no one can ever be sure what goes on in the minds of sheep.

"Tell us another story papa!" The girl said.

"Shush, he didn't finish this one!" Said the little boy.

A door opened from a small cottage made entirely of rock, a beautiful woman walked up the hill where her family sat, and she brought tea and flat bread. Behind her a melfling closely followed.

"Well now, Robert is right. I didn't finish the story. Thomas sailed the ocean for many months…searching for his love, Aurella. He searched for her long and far and at times things were very hard, but he never gave up. He fought off the pirates of Sairbon and the wild folk of Nor F'olan and survived. He had the magic compass in his possession so he always knew what direction she lay."

"Tell us about the pirates!" Said the little girl.

"Another time, Zoe, another time. Let me finish this story."

Zoe made a scrunch face but smiled at her papa.

"Thomas found Aurella, and convinced her of his love…and they lived happily together to the end of days."

"What happened to the dragon?" Asked Robert.

"He's still out there, beware."

"Tell us another story papa!" Shouted Zoe hugging Moshki at the same time.

"Enough stories." Aurella said, "It's off to bed with the both of you."

Thomas smiled at Aurella, and pulled out the compass in his pocket reading it.

"This still points to you." He said.

"Don't ever lose me again."

CPSIA information can be obtained
at www.ICGtesting.com
Printed in the USA
FFOW02n0926120117
31129FF